'You know, when you turned up in that pool, I'd been sitting there wishing something unusual would happen in my life, something new and——'

Misty said dully, 'You really don't know what you're saying. I live in another world, Mr Turner. I play detective games for a living, and I don't have any background at all. I don't know how to be a hostess, and I can't talk cooking and exotic dinner dishes. I don't know my wines and I don't know who my ancestors were. I hate parties, and I——' Oh, lord! Why had she said all that? As if she—as if he——

'Easy, Misty Dawn.' Zeb's thumbs were moving again, caressing the tension away from her neck. 'I won't rush you. Maybe this is a crazy insanity I'm feeling, but...' His lips were suddenly there, brushing her open mouth, leaving her tingling and trembling. 'I don't think so,' he whispered. 'But we'll find out, won't we? Tomorrow... and the next day... and the next.'

TAKING CHANCES

BY
VANESSA GRANT

MILLS & BOON LIMITED
ETON HOUSE   18-24 PARADISE ROAD
RICHMOND   SURREY   TW9 1SR

First published in Great Britain 1989
by Mills & Boon Limited

© Vanessa Grant 1989

Australian copyright 1989
Philippine copyright 1989
This edition 1989

ISBN 0 263 76494 X

Set in Times Roman 10 on 12 pt.
01-8912-55611 C

Made and printed in Great Britain

This book is dedicated to Janet Norman
in fond memory of one day in Kitimat
and an idea that got changed in the telling

CHAPTER ONE

MISTY pushed the button two minutes after Zebediah Turner sat down in an uncomfortable chair by the window. It was simply instinct.

She sat down when he did. She crossed her legs and adjusted her pleated skirt smoothly to avoid showing her knees. She leaned back in her chair and waited to see if he would speak first. She knew the image she projected: small and blonde and fluffy. All her life men had been underestimating her because of her tiny good looks. She had learned not to resent it. In her line of work it was an advantage to have hidden skills.

This man might be more perceptive than most. He was watching her rather closely, but he might not realise that she was aware of every move he made. If she had to, she could describe him in court. Six feet tall. Broad shoulders that didn't need a skilled tailor to fill them out. He had the kind of build that sometimes concealed surprising strength. Greenish eyes. Brown hair brushed into tameness. A face that barely escaped classic handsomeness, that had faint lines, as if he had lived a little too hard in his—what? Forty years? He knew he was attractive to women. It was in the smile, in the way he held his body when he sat; reinforced by the slightly cynical light in his greenish eyes. She gave him a moment to realise that the chair was truly uncomfortable.

'Well, Mr Turner, what can I do for you?'

'Zeb,' he corrected, smiling. He used that smile a lot.

She smiled back, despite the warning tingle she felt. It was part of the game. Sometimes her work was more like acting than detective work, and she liked that. When she was acting she could feel strong and confident and skilful. None of her insecurities showed.

He was hesitating, but she smiled again and waited for him to talk first. Uncle Kenny had taught her—keep silent, let them commit themselves first, keep the advantage.

'I thought I would be seeing Mr Donovan.' He toyed with the arm of the chair, his eyes a little left of hers. 'I made an appointment with Kenneth Donovan.'

She frowned, her instincts alert. Did he want something that Uncle Kenny might consent to, but she might not? 'We're *partners*, Mr Turner. Donovan and Donovan, Private Detectives. At the moment Mr Donovan is not available. My secretary assumed that you would be willing to see the other partner. If you'd like to wait until next week——'

'No! I——' For the first time, he looked disconcerted. 'I can't wait that long.'

'Then——?' she prompted patiently. Nothing on earth would induce her to admit that Uncle Kenny had disappeared last week, that she had no idea where he might be or when he would return.

Mr Turner was taking his time getting to the point. She was a little startled to realise that she couldn't help liking this man, despite the fact that she was sure no one in their right minds should trust him an inch.

'I'm a writer,' he said finally, very smoothly, pulling the chair a little closer to her desk. He was lying. His hands were oddly restless on the arm of the chair as he said, 'And I've got a rather odd job for you.'

'Yes?' That was when she pushed the button. Her blue eyes held his hazel-green ones and he didn't see her finger move, but every word he said, every smile, would now be recorded on film. Thankfully the camera made no sound. When Uncle Kenny had first installed it, it had been subject to fits of noisy activity. Misty had refused to use it for months.

She glanced down at her desk, realised that she been absently doodling, sketching a caricature of the man. High forehead. Lean face. Same for the body—long and lean. Everything about his clothing was conservative, yet she could have sworn that his natural dress would be more dramatic, almost flamboyant. Funny, the man's personality did not quite match his carefully considered wardrobe.

'You wouldn't be more comfortable in the other chair?' she asked him innocently, nodding towards the large, overstuffed chair that attracted most of her clients. She enjoyed watching people choose their seating. He had chosen the uncomfortable seat. Why? Because he did not want to be observed too closely?

'No, thank you.' He shifted, arranged his legs, one crossed casually over the other at the ankle. It was a pose that seemed awkward on him. It was intended to be unstudied, but did not quite make it. Amateur theatre, she decided. All his friends must have told him what a good actor he was.

'A writer?' she murmured, pleased to see a slight discomfort cross his face. No doubt about it. He *was* lying.

'Yes,' he agreed quickly. 'A writer. I—well, I'm not published yet. I'm a shipbuilder by trade.' The smile flashed. 'I'm writing at nights, trying to create a best-selling mystery novel.'

A shipbuilder. She had seen a sign painted on the side
of a building down by the waterfront. Beside the caricature face she wrote 'Turner Enterprises'. She saw his
mask slip just a fraction to reveal what she could have
sworn was the look of a petulant small boy. 'I have a
publisher interested in this book proposal.' Did he want
her to write the book for him? 'Research,' he said
abruptly, then he seemed to recover his poise and he
smiled at her. If she'd been susceptible, her heart would
have smashed into her ribcage. 'I came for some help
with the research.'

She drew a line under the face and the name of the
business. 'Research is certainly the business we're in, but
not usually——'

'I want you to kidnap me.'

She managed to keep her face still, although her fingers
twitched, reaching for the camera button before her mind
could catch up and remember she had already started
the film moving. The man was insane, out of his flaming
head! Kidnap him? Damn Kenny! He'd disappeared last
week, and now she had a maniac to contend with, alone.

Typical. Despite Kenny, she had always faced everything alone.

'Kidnapping,' she said lightly. 'We don't get that one
every day.'

'No, I don't suppose so.' He laughed, and she had
that odd feeling that he was acting again. 'You see, my
hero is a kidnap victim, and I'm having trouble with
chapters two and three. I need to get into his point of
view, you see, and I don't really—well, I've just never
been kidnapped.'

'So you want me to do it for you?' This would be a
wild tale to tell Kenny when he finally turned up. 'How
would you like it done? At the point of a gun?' Misty

had a gun, on Uncle Kenny's insistence, but she never carried it. 'I'm afraid I'm not going to take on that one, Mr Turner. Kidnapping is a felony, you know, and——'

He leaned forward earnestly. 'But this is really just a game. I need to get the setting right to——' He spread his arms engagingly. 'I know it sounds wild, but what I need is someone to play the part of kidnapper, so I can play the part of my hero and get the feel for the situation. It would take twenty-four hours of your time, and of course I'll pay whatever your going rate is for this sort of thing.'

'This sort of thing?' she repeated, bemused. 'I don't think this is on our fee schedule.' She sat up and her chair made a faint noise as the spring pushed the back erect. 'You need an actress, Mr Turner. You want someone to play a part.'

Then he said, 'I'll pay five thousand dollars,' and she thought about Uncle Kenny being missing and wondered how badly in debt he would be when he returned.

By midnight on a week-night it was rare for anyone to be using the whirlpool or the swimming pool. That was why Zeb Turner chose that time for his nightly swim. It was a habit that everyone knew—the guard at the gate, the bartender in the clubhouse. The caretaker made an extra round of the spa facilities just before midnight every weekday, checking for anything out of place before the boss found it.

The spa had been built for the marina's customers, part of the luxurious facilities that encouraged well-off 'live-aboards' to keep their boats at the Turner marina. Running a marina went with having a shipyard, and there was certainly a tendency for the people who used the marina to go to the Turner shipyard for their haul-outs and repairs.

Six years ago, when Zeb had proposed using some of the land attached to the Turner mansion for a recreation facility, Neil had accused him of catering exclusively to the wealthy. There was some truth in his younger brother's accusation. When their father had died, Zeb had taken over a family of dependants. He looked after them well, making certain the company remained profitable as it grew.

Yet, much as he loved his family, in the middle of the night, when the shipyard and his family were all sleeping, he always slipped away to spend an hour swimming hard and relaxing. He was always careful to lock the doors behind him before he walked down the path and let himself through the locked gate that separated his grounds from the marina. As part of the nightly ritual, he would lift his hand in a silent greeting to the guard at the gate of the car park. The guard always returned the greeting.

Inside the spa compound he would strip off his towelling robe and toss it on to a deck-chair beside the pool, then dive in and swim length after length until he was exhausted. The water soothed away the tensions of a day spent sitting at a desk. The swimming stretched and exercised muscles knotted from too many hours in the office. The pool, indirectly lit by the dim glow from the lights over the car park, seemed shrouded in a private peace.

As always, on Monday night he swam hard for twenty minutes, then turned and did a slow, steady backstroke. He let the energy flow back into his body, let his eyes and his mind focus on the big palm tree that loomed over the far end of the pool. The palm tree was always there, a soothing giant in the night. He swam until the tree was high overhead, its leaves drooping down over the pool, filling his sky. In the instant before the concrete edge of the pool touched his head, he turned and began to swim back. Over his head, only the brightest stars penetrated the city lights.

For a moment his solitude seemed like loneliness, then he pushed the fancy away. If he went to the telephone in the guard's shack and called Alice, she would be with him in half an hour. He did not call. He never shared this nightly ritual with anyone else. Instead he shook off the mood and swung up a metal ladder. Water streamed off his lean body as he walked past his robe and into the room where the whirlpool steamed, quietly inactive. His fingers found the switch on the wall and flicked it up. There was a rumble, a roar, then the water began to bubble. He stepped down two steps and the pounding hot water enveloped him.

A few minutes later one of the waiters from the club came out carrying a tall tumbler. It was the same drink they brought him every night. Easy on the Scotch. Lots of ginger ale. Ice tinkling in the glass.

'Thanks,' he said, his words hardly penetrating the noisy water, but the waiter nodded and grinned and left him alone. Alone. Curious how alone he had felt lately. He was surrounded by family, had a satisfactory lover. He had just turned forty years old last week and he had accomplished all the things he had dreamed of when he'd taken over his father's business as a very young man. There was no reason for him to feel this childish yearning for something *exciting* to walk into his life. No reason at all.

He pushed the haunting sensation away and ticked off his obligations mentally as the hot water swirled around him. This was part of his daily ritual to ensure that he hadn't forgotten to deal with any of the many.

His mother. She had telephoned from Phoenix that morning, complaining that her car was in the garage and she couldn't get home in time for the meeting. He had suppressed a pleasant fantasy of an annual meeting without her demands and told his secretary to arrange a plane ticket for his mother, and a driver to bring the car back to San Diego when it was repaired.

Helen, his sister-in-law. She had not received her alimony cheque from Barry this month. Not unusual, but it seemed that Julian, her son, had to go to the orthodontist, an expensive proposition. Zeb had told her to send him the bill, promised to get on Barry's case about the alimony and had written out a cheque to tide her over.

What about Julian? He frowned, fighting the relaxing action of the water. No, there was nothing he could pin down, but perhaps he should take Julian out next weekend, try to get a feel for the boy's state of mind. These young boys got complicated when they hit their teens, and problems could develop quickly. Look at Keith, Neil's son! For years everything had been smooth between the boy and his father, then last year Keith had exploded in an adolescent rebellion that had resulted in his moving in with Zeb while the father-son relationship cooled off.

At least Keith was doing well. His maths teacher had called the office today to tell Zeb he wanted to put Keith into the Mathematics League contest. And the boy was on speaking terms with Neil again.

Neil himself was in Canada right now. There wasn't much Zeb could do about that except hope his younger brother worked out his problems. Neil went his own way, looked after himself. He was the only member of the family who did not lean on Zeb. But surely he would pay heed to Zeb's warning and get back in time for the meeting on Wednesday?

What about Barry? Wasn't it time for Barry to get into some new financial jam? He pushed Barry's image aside and tried to relax. He could hear nothing, just the water, but he felt the intrusion and his eyes opened.

There was bubbling water all around him, flooding out any other noises...the car park seen dimly through the glass...the swimming pool through the open doorway, still and empty...and there, at the doorway to the spa, a woman, small and blonde. Not beautiful, he decided, but very attractive, pretty with those blonde curls and that air of fragility. Something familiar in the way she walked towards the whirlpool. There would be a man not far behind her. She was the kind of woman who always had a man hovering, holding doors and looking after her.

The noise of the water made it easy not to say hello to her. He closed his eyes again and went on down a mental list of jobs to be done at the office tomorrow. Reschedule the Peters job. Then call the yard foreman into his office the try to get to the bottom of the rumours he'd been hearing. Although his eyes were closed, he was aware of her presence in a way that he found uncomfortable. He lifted the glass and sipped without looking at her. The ice was almost all gone, but the liquid was a welcome coolness along his throat.

It would be insane to say that he felt the disturbance in the water when she stepped into the whirlpool. The water was bubbling, roaring in a turmoil created by the powerful pump housed in a room not fifty feet from them. He opened his eyes and she was there, across from him, the water slipping up her tanned body as she sank down.

She was someone's guest. She belonged to one of the playboys who rotated women each month. Yes, he decided, his mind rejecting the appeal of her shapely, slender body. He closed his eyes, but her image was vividly painted on the back of his eyelids. How could he have memorised her shape so quickly? Her bathing-suit was one piece and technically modest, yet mysteriously alluring in the way it covered her. It was November, but she was tanned a silky warm gold that glistened against her blonde curls.

He opened his eyes, felt the shock of meeting hers. No, not a playboy's toy. She was different. And he had seen her before, but where?

The timer went off. Silence grew as the water stilled. Intimacy, abrupt and uncomfortable. No one else in the world but himself and this woman who was a stranger. Her lips parted in preparation for speech. He tensed, a cautionary voice urging him to leave before she could be a danger to him. No wonder he didn't have adventures like his brothers! He was programmed to avoid them, to be the stable one.

Before he could move or the woman talk, the guard at the gate came in, an envelope in his hand. 'Telegram Mr Turner. Just phoned into the clubhouse.' The guard's eyes took in the woman, politely avoided staring at the slight swelling above the bodice of her blue bathing-suit, at the shadow that caught Zeb's eyes where her cleavage disappeared into the blue.

Damn! He could not seem to stop reacting to her. She shifted and leaned back against the wall of the pool. He felt his body respond to her motions. It would be impossible for him to stand up and walk away until either she was gone, or his male hormones had backed down.

'Open it for me, would you, Harry? My hands are wet.' His voice was casual, as if his body weren't heating up like a teenager's. Lord! How long had it been since he'd spent a night with Alice? Too long, he supposed, or this would not be happening.

The envelope was neatly ripped open and the paper inside spread out and in Zeb's fingers. Before he looked at it he remembered to ask, 'How's your wife doing? And the baby?'

'Fine,' said Harry, smiling with pleasure. 'The baby's nine pounds already.'

He could feel her watching. She was not the light-weight pretty lady he had thought in that first instant, although he was damned if he could tell just what she was. 'Want me to start the water again?' asked Harry as he left.

'Please,' agreed Zeb, and the water turned wild again. At least now when he looked at her he could not see the reflections, the hints of her slender legs, her arms smoothing out the water around her.

Who was she?

The telegram was from his brother, and he couldn't help smiling when he read it. Neil had flown north a week ago, his mind in turmoil as he finally gave in to his feelings for the Canadian woman he had fallen in love with so dramatically. Now the telegram announced, 'Flying in for AGM Wednesday early. Don't worry. I won't be late. Wedding at Christmas so don't make any other plans for December. Serena sends her love to Keith. Break the news to Mother. Love Neil.'

Signing a letter or a telegram with 'love' was really not in character for his impulsive but emotionally restrained younger brother. That repression of emotions was one of the things that had created problems between Neil and his son, one of the reasons Keith was staying with Zeb this year. Serena had obviously affected his brother at a very deep level, and Zeb was glad because Neil was the one person in the family whose problems he had never been able to do much about.

He took advantage of the distraction of Neil's telegram to get out of the whirlpool while his response to the woman was dormant. He dived into the swimming pool and swam hard. For years there had been only Alice, a romantic friendship that was enough for both of them, safe for both of them. He really wanted nothing more. He was not about to take the risks of promiscuity in this day and age.

She was still there when he finished the last length and pushed himself out of the pool with a strong surge of his arms. He came to his feet on the tiled border of the pool, reached for his robe, and could see her in the whirlpool, waiting for him.

His routine was inviolate. He swam, then relaxed in the whirlpool, then swam again, cooling off. Then he went for a shower before he walked home. Tonight, he found himself breaking the pattern, walking back towards the woman, the robe trailing from his hand until he dropped it on the chair beside her.

She was still sitting on the ledge that provided a comfortable seat under the water. She had not turned the timer back on, so it was very quiet. Her damp arms were spread back along the edge of the pool and he could see that she had slender, strong muscles. She kept herself fit somehow. Tennis? Or was she one of those women who worked out with weights? Alice was too restrained to get into activities that worked up a sweat. Zeb found himself wondering what a woman like this would be like in his bed—lean and strong, with surprisingly soft, womanly curves.

The fantastic thought brought an instant reaction to his body. He saw her eyes jerk away from him. He felt a sharp excitement at her unexpected shyness. He stood still, watching her, not trying to hide what she had already seen. He found her a very desirable woman. He wondered what her voice would be like, and when it came it was husky and yet strong.

'Mr Turner, I don't know what your game is, but I'm not playing.'

He blinked, running the words back the way he did in a risky business contact, making sure he had taken in all the implications before he replied. Then he smiled, because he liked her voice. 'Run that by me again. I think I missed something.'

'You know what I'm talking about.' Her eyes met his now, cool and challenging. 'I've been following you for the last forty-eight hours. I don't suppose you expected me to do that, but it's only common sense.'

He had the feeling that he had wandered into another dimension, as if this were one of those nonsensical science fiction novels where the hero walked into an insane world and never found his way back home. 'Common sense?' he repeated. She seemed totally at ease now, although only a moment ago her face had flushed brilliantly at his response to her woman's curves.

'Of course,' she said coolly. He watched her hands settle on her hips under the water. 'You didn't think I'd just take your money and do what you want without a second thought, did you?'

'Take my money?' For what? What was it she had said? Do what he wanted? He wanted—surely she did not mean the hot, lustful images growing in his mind? He felt his face flushing, as if she could see his thoughts.

'Did you think I was gullible, that I wouldn't check up on you?' She smiled wryly. 'I suppose you thought I was a dumb blonde, but I'm quite intelligent.'

'That I never doubted.' Her intelligence was in her eyes, in the way she moved with purpose. 'Who are you? You've been following me?'

'Every minute,' she said grimly.

He grinned suddenly and said, 'I can't imagine it was very interesting for you. Much more exciting for me, knowing that you bothered. What did you learn?'

She shook the damp curls back. Her voice lost its heat, became businesslike. 'That you're too busy being Mr Responsible to take time to write an off-beat mystery novel.' He said nothing. He was too astounded, and she had more to say. She spread her fingers, ticking off items. 'Your mother is stranded in Phoenix with a sick car. Your girlfriend needs help buying a new property. You're supporting one brother's ex-wife and son, and you've got your other brother's son living with you. You took him to a football game last night, and you've curtailed your dates with your girlfriend to be home for the kid every night. And you've got union problems.'

'The union problems aren't serious.' The words left his lips without his thinking.

She shook her head. 'They might be. That new ship-wright you took on is spreading discontent. If you don't deal with him you'll have a strike before the year's over.'

'Who the hell are you?' Malenski. That was the new shipwright's name, and he could picture the man as an agitator.

She stood up, stepped quickly up to the deck around the whirlpool, the water forming drops on her arms and legs. Her hair was damp, curling a little more from the steamy air than it had been when he'd first seen her. She was slightly taller than he had thought, but she had to tip her head back to look him in the eyes. He wondered who the hell she was and why she made his heart pound as if he'd found something magic. He was too old for magic spells.

She said, 'I'm supposed to be here, aren't I?' She smiled when he shook his head. 'Yes, I know. Tomorrow, you said, but I'm not going to play, Mr Turner. I don't know what your plan was, what the scheme was, but you lied to me.'

His smile died and he said rigidly. 'Lady, whoever you are, I've never seen you before in my life.' He remembered now, and he said, 'No, I've seen you. Last night, at the football game. You were there.' He'd had just a glimpse, a tiny blonde woman, all curls and quick movements.

'I was there,' she agreed. 'But it was you who came to my office Saturday with that ridiculous proposition. I admit that the money is tempting, but we're turning it down.'

'The money? We?' She was very serious. Her eyes persuaded him that this was not a practical joke. 'Who is we?'

She jerked her head. 'Neither of us is interested in taking on your job. As I suggested on Saturday, if you're really going to pursue this, try an actor.'

This was going from crazy to screwball. He found himself shouting, 'Are you nuts?' as she bent to pick up her towel. 'Lady, who the hell are you?'

She tossed her head back and he could see the anger flash in her eyes as she said tightly, 'Listen, I don't need this. I'm doing you the courtesy of letting you know that you're wasting your time with me. I know you're a game player. I could see that when you came into my office.'

'A game player?' He kept repeating the words she said. He felt like an actor who did not know the lines.

She draped the big beach towel around her shoulders. It hung to her knees and covered all the female curves. She looked very young with the woman hidden away under the terry cloth. Some part of his mind wondered who looked after her, and something in her eyes seemed to tell him that no one did. Then she stepped towards him and he found himself automatically stepping back, a gentleman's gesture to give her room.

'I can't figure you out,' she said as she passed him, her eyes going to his face. He saw the shyness flash in their blue depths before she suppressed it and said, 'I know it's some kind of a scam. So I'm warning you. I've got Saturday on tape. Every word.'

'On tape?' He wanted to reach out and hold her back, but he had never laid a restraining hand on a woman in his life, except for that night when Helen had had hysterics when she'd learned that Barry was chasing everything in skirts. 'On tape?' he repeated, alarmed and not understanding why. 'Just what the hell have you got on tape?' Saturday? What had he done Saturday? The office. An afternoon visit to Alice. Surely she didn't have a camera in Alice's apartment? 'What in hell is going on?' he demanded, stepping towards her.

She stepped back as he advanced, her hands lifting, her voice suddenly hard. 'Don't try anything, Mr Turner. I'm not nearly as helpless as I look. And don't forget that videotape. Every word you said is on it. I don't know what the scam is. It *sounded* screwy as hell, but after following you for a day I know damned well you're not screwy. There's some reason, and I don't really care what it is, but just leave me out of it.'

She was going, and he was totally at sea, could only watch as her hips swung away from him, revealed by the swinging towel. Then abruptly, she turned back. 'You'd better do something about your nephew.' Her eyes had lost their anger. She was outside the whirlpool room, standing exposed to the night air. He could see her shiver slightly in the bathing-suit and bare feet. 'He needs help,' she said, her voice suddenly husky.

'My nephew? Keith?' There was something about her warning that he could not ignore.

'No. Julian. He's getting into a bad scene with his school chums.'

Zeb frowned. Who was she? How did she know all the details of his life? Alice and Mother and Helen and Keith. And now Julian. 'What kind of bad scene?'

'Drugs.' She saw his sudden frown, said, 'I don't know how deep he is, but his buddies are in deep. The guy with the tattoo on his arm is the ringleader.' He was frowning and she smiled suddenly. 'You'll handle it,' she said wryly. 'It's what you do, isn't it? You know, I came here figuring you were some kind of con artist pulling a business stunt of some kind. But it's not that, is it?'

He shook his head in bewilderment, not agreement. She said, 'I thought not. Good luck with the union. And the nephew.'

She was gone, not to the changing-rooms, but straight out to the car park and into a white Corvette that started with a quiet roar and sped away towards the guard house. Who the hell was she? How would he find her again without a telephone number or even a name?

CHAPTER TWO

WHEN she'd driven into the complex, the guard at the gate had not prevented her entry. He had stopped her car, and she had smiled and let him take in her fluffy blondeness. 'Zeb Turner's expecting me,' she had said, deliberately mixing boldness with a slight embarrassment.

She had dressed in a sexy blue swimming-suit that was not quite concealed by the big white towel draped over her shoulders. The suit covered her quite modestly, but she knew that it hinted at every curve she possessed and was actually more erotic than a skimpy bikini would have been. She hadn't blushed. This was business, and her private shyness never showed when she was working. She simply let the guard come to the obvious conclusion, and she filed away his surprise. So it was unusual for Zeb to meet a woman here. It seemed that he was faithful to his mistress.

'Mr Turner didn't——' he'd begun uneasily, but she had said hurriedly,

'You're not going to make me wait out here, are you? I'm cold. Zeb said the pool was warm, but——' She'd smiled and shivered and he'd waved her in, forgetting that he had asked for her pass only moments ago.

She had intended to confront Zeb Turner in the pool where he would be off guard, to tell him she hadn't fallen for his story. Only, when she arrived in the whirlpool, he had not seemed off guard at all. She had been the one disconcerted. Somehow the man's presence had packed a sensual impact that he had not had for her on

Saturday. And now, driving away in her wet bathing-suit, she was more confused than ever. Disturbing. She had no idea what it was about, and mysteries bothered her terribly. It was one of the reasons she did well as a detective, because her mind worried and worried at mysteries until she found some way to get at the truth hidden under the surface.

She did not believe that he was writing a book. The notion was far-fetched, did not fit the man she had just left in the whirlpool. He was a strong, conventional and direct man. His world was as far from her own crazy world of stealth and deceit as it could be.

It simply did not add up. What possible motive could there be for that insane request that she kidnap him? It had made only minimal sense on Saturday, even less sense when she'd started following him. She had found herself spying on the life of an honourable man, and yet—what about Saturday?

Everything she learned conflicted with that visit he had made to her office. It was as if there were two men. The one on the videotape, and the one she had followed and confronted in the whirlpool. She wished he had told her what it was really about. She drove out through the gates, smiled at the guard and waved, and tried not to admit to herself how much it bothered her that she was never going to know the answers to her questions.

Tonight, his eyes had watched her in a different way. The man himself had seemed different. Cool. No, she thought, flushing with the memory, not cool. She had seen his response to her. Yet even that was confusing, this chemistry. How could she meet him on Saturday, sharing that strange conversation without any feel of chemistry between them, and then tonight——? On Saturday she had liked him, felt a warmth tempered strongly with suspicion, not unlike the feelings she had for her uncle. Tonight——

Her mind spun, trying to make sense of one man who could be two such different people. The Corvette ate up the miles once she turned on to the freeway, but even the fast driving could not clear her mind enough to make sense of it. She pulled off the freeway, along a secondary access road, and she still felt a frustrated curiosity.

She let her low-slung car bump gently over the place which she would eventually have to get professionally levelled, then pulled over the top of the small hill and coasted down to park outside a high white wall that concealed her private waterfront yard. Behind the wall was a small house, smaller than it looked from the red tile roof that was visible from the road. Much of the room inside was taken up by a covered patio at the back. She opened the car door and she could hear Max, one sharp bark and then the scrabble of his paws on the inside of the gate.

'Hold on, Max!' He stilled when he heard her voice. She opened the gate, smiling, welcoming the Dobermann's rush towards her. He was excitable and affectionate, not unlike a small, irrepressible child.

'Easy, Max.' She bent to scratch him behind the pointed ear that twitched erect when he heard noises in the night. His fur felt glossy and clean, and she stroked him, enjoying the sensation on her palm. 'We'll eat,' she promised, walking hunched over in order to keep scratching him, then fitting her key into the front door of the house. He had his bowl of dry dog food, but she knew he was waiting for the treat she would produce for him now that she was home. 'Then we'll walk on the beach.' His ears pointed high at the word 'walk.' He

enjoyed their midnight walks as much as she did. Tonight she was late, but he had waited as he always did.

The inside of her house was a big, round, open space
with her bedroom leading off one side, her bathroom
off the bedroom. The kitchen and living area were div-
ided with hanging beads that gave the effect of walls
without destroying the open spaciousness. The décor was
simple, somewhat Mexican in tone. She had no money
for expensive pictures, but Mexican blankets made
colourful wall-hangings against the white walls, and set
off the natural varnished wood around the ceiling and
windows. The floor was tiled with the same warm brown
ceramic tiles that were on the patio, with colourful area
rugs here and there. She liked the house. It was small,
but it was hers, and it felt warm and friendly to her.

She went first to the telephone answering machine,
but there was no message light glowing, no word from
Kenny. She would not let herself be disappointed. He
would show up eventually. She went to the kitchen and
got a bone for Max and a small container of yoghurt
for herself. Then, while Max gnawed on the bone, she
ate and doodled on a piece of paper at the kitchen-table.

She changed into shorts and T-shirt after she ate. It
was the middle of the night, almost winter, but she was
seldom cold. She had been born in the north, and the
hardiness born of cold winters was still with her. A
November night in southern California was no reason
to pile on winter clothes. She and Max walked the dark
beach as always, alone and enjoying each other's
company. Yet somehow tonight the walk failed to ease
her restlessness.

Later, she dreamed about him—the man in the
whirlpool, not the one in her office. She woke in the
dark, her heart thundering in her ears. As she sat up in

bed, Max came scrambling to his feet and tore into the bedroom, as if she had cried out.

'It's nothing, you idiot!' she told him. 'Go back to sleep.' He stared at her, whimpered once, then turned and walked away with his head hanging. She pressed her hand against the skin between her breasts, felt her body shuddering, her breasts swollen with the dream. What on earth had got into her to create a sleeping fantasy like that?

She tried to sleep again, half afraid the sensuous dream would return. She was still awake when dawn came, her mind fighting with a crazy mystery she would probably never solve. Kenny would understand, she thought wryly. Her uncle could seldom leave a mystery untouched. She had earned his respect, if not his love, by learning to be better at digging out facts and truths than Kenny had ever been.

Not that Kenny wasn't good. He had been a private detective since she was small. She thought she remembered a time when he had been a policeman, but she wasn't sure and she would never know now. Kenny never talked about his past, and she knew better than to ask. She loved him intensely and was careful never to show it, and she knew that if she walked out of his life he would miss her work more than her person.

She could remember being very small, riding her tricycle down the driveway, careening straight into Uncle Kenny, staring up and laughing because he was her favourite—her *only* uncle. With the treachery of childhood memories, she did not remember the other details. Her parents had not been there, the shadowy mother and father. There must have been a baby-sitter around, or a neighbour, but she could not remember. She remembered Kenny's face staring down. He had not laughed back, and she remembered her joy turning to fear.

There had been that long silence. She had been frozen on the tricycle, staring up, the fear growing until he finally said, 'Well, Misty Dawn, you'd better come with me.' It was the last time he had ever used her father's nickname for her.

She had followed him, walking away from everything, not looking back because something in his face forbade it. She had never seen the tricycle again, or the house. Even now, twenty years later, she did not know what had happened to her parents. She thought it was a car accident, but Kenny had never said, and you simply did not probe for details if Uncle Kenny did not want to talk. She had only asked him once. She never asked again.

He had sent her to a boarding-school. She remembered being the smallest, the youngest, crying alone at night in the strange bed. She had come to Kenny in the holidays. There were no other relatives. Her memories of those first couple of summers were hazy, mostly memories of the string of Kenny's girlfriends who did most of the work of looking after a little girl during holiday time.

For some reason Kenny had no girlfriend the summer Misty was eight years old. Misty and Kenny were alone in the apartment through the summer, the girl sleeping on the sofa and her uncle behind the bedroom door. One evening she somehow managed to get out the words.

'Uncle Kenny, what happened to Mommy and Daddy? Are they dead?' In school, she had been asked to make up a family tree. She had been unable to answer so many of the questions. The need to know had become more immediate and painful.

He had not answered. He had gone pale, then his face had grown hard with that look, shutting her out. There had been a long, heavy silence. She had lifted her hands, fingers out, as if she could grasp her own words and pull them back, un-say them.

The door had slammed when he'd left the apartment. She had lain awake all night, listening for him to return, lying under the covers so that he would think she was sleeping when he did come in. He had not come, and she had not slept.

She had not been allowed to call the office where he worked, so she'd waited, terrified, watching the telephone that did not ring and the door that did not open. It had been a week before he'd returned. The last two days before he'd come back, she had had nothing to eat.

He'd returned in the middle of the night, on the eighth night. She'd pretended to sleep and he had gone directly into his room. The next morning he had taken her out to breakfast, then for the first time he'd taken her to the office with him.

It was the beginning of another world for her, an exciting world of mysteries and adventure. They never mentioned the week he had left her alone. When they talked, it was about work. She was good at following people. No one ever suspected that the cute blonde kid was part of Donovan's Detective Agency. She learned how to find out things—telephone books and directories and government register offices. She learned how to ask questions about people without sounding as if the answers mattered. By the time she was fourteen she knew more about being a detective than most people learned in a lifetime, and she loved it. When she did a good job at the agency, Kenny looked happy.

She was a quick learner, and with Kenny she had to be. He was taciturn when it came to personal matters, so she learned to read his signals, to avoid actions that would send him out of the door. He disappeared again from time to time. She tried never to give him cause, but sometimes he would turn grey and hard, and when the door slammed she knew she would be alone until he came back. Each time he left, something shrivelled up inside her, but she never went hungry again. She kept a secret stash of money for food, and she learned to handle the detective agency when he left.

When she graduated, he insisted she go to university and she did not argue. Her first year at Berkeley was endless—months of lonely misery. She did well enough in her classes, but she was lonely and would have cried herself to sleep if she had not learned years ago not to cry, no matter what. Kenny did not like tears.

She spent the next summer being Kenny's right hand again, but did not ask to stay when September came. She knew better.

She met Wayne on her first day back at university... He had stepped on her instep in the bookstore, his big, muscular frame painfully heavy on her small foot. He had apologised, and she had grinned at the sincere agony in his face.

'It doesn't matter,' she had insisted. 'I'm tough. It takes more than that to finish me off.'

He had not believed that, although it was more than true. 'Come on,' he had insisted urgently. 'I'll buy you a drink. You can get off your feet; you really should rest that foot for a bit.'

No one had ever fussed over her like that, not since a shadowy mother. She had let him lead her away, and in a quiet, pretty cocktail lounge he had pumped her without finding out much about the tiny blonde girl except that they shared a sociology class.

He had pursued her, refusing to listen when she said 'no' to an invitation to go dancing. He was gentle with her, oddly reverent of her smallness. He had made her feel cherished and wanted. She'd fallen in love with a frightening intensity. It had lasted almost a year. When it had ended, she had left the university, returned to Kenny's apartment unannounced. There had been a girl staying with Kenny, and Misty had felt horribly alone and unwelcome. At the office the next day, she had said nervously, 'I'm not going back to university.'

He had said nothing and she had gulped, afraid he would walk out and disappear again, leaving her more alone than she had ever been in her life. She'd said hesitantly, 'If you don't want me working here, I can get a job at the bank. I—I think I can get a job as a teller trainee.'

Kenny had not looked up from his papers. His voice had sounded coldly angry. 'That would be a stupid waste of your intelligence, just because your first love affair went wrong.'

So even Wayne had not been a secret from Kenny. She knew that was the way he looked after her, but she felt an invasion of her privacy, yet pain because she could not share her disillusionment with him. 'You'd better find yourself somewhere to live,' he had growled as he'd walked out, and she had moved into her own apartment a week later.

One day a sign painter had arrived and changed the name over the door to 'Donovan and Donovan'. Her income had gone up too, and down during the bad months. She had become a partner in every sense of the word. She had tried to tell herself that it meant he wanted her. She'd also tried to tell herself that she liked living alone in her cold little apartment.

She had found Max a few years later during a rather frightening case Kenny had taken on. The client had been an insurance company, and Misty had done most of the leg work. She had found the evidence required to defeat a rather complex insurance scam. The author of the scam had run away to Canada and left behind one five-year-old Dobermann pinscher dog. The man had finally been extradited from Canada and sent to jail in California, but no one had known what to do with the dog. The neighbours had not wanted it. There was no one else.

Misty smuggled Max into her apartment building, only to receive an eviction notice herself within a week. She took the dog to work.

'I have to rent a house,' she had told Kenny when he'd stared at the dog the next morning. 'Some place that doesn't mind a dog.' Max had growled and Kenny had glared. 'He doesn't like men much,' she had explained quickly. 'I think his owner treated him badly.'

'Better buy your own place,' Kenny had said finally. 'You're gonna have nothing but hassles renting.'

'Buy?' She'd swung her legs around and risen from the wheeled office chair she liked to use. 'With what for money?'

He had stared at her with the look she associated with his frequent disappearances, then growled, 'The money your parents left you. Use it.'

Until that day, she'd had no idea that she had any resources except for her clothes and her books and the white Corvette she loved...and Max. The money, it turned out, was in trust until she reached twenty-five. She was twenty-three then, but Uncle Kenny had been the trustee, and it seemed it had been no problem to release funds to put a down-payment on the small house.

So she and Max had moved into their new home, and life had taken on a depth that had not been there before. She had discovered that, although she had never learned much about being domestic, she and a dark, vicious-looking dog could make a warm home together. It wasn't often that she felt dissatisfied. Nights like the one she had just spent were rare. She had read articles that claimed a modern woman could make a happy life alone, and she believed it was true.

She shook off Zeb's uncomfortable presence in her mind and got ready for work. She steeled herself against the single whimper Max made. He would spend the day chasing waves on the beach, lazing in the sun on the patio. 'I'll be back,' she promised him as she closed the gate and got into the Corvette.

There was no word from Kenny at the office. 'But someone's looking for him,' announced Jo-Anne, the secretary. She had been pounding away at the typewriter when Misty came in, had stopped instantly to take her glasses off and squint up at Misty. Misty could never decide if Jo-Anne actually needed glasses or not. There was no real pattern to the times she put them on and took them off. Now she was squinting, making lines in her chubby, good-natured face, saying, 'The man who called claims—half in Spanish and half in English—that he bought a car from Kenny in Acapulco and there's something wrong with the papers.'

Misty winced and Jo-Anne looked angry. 'He should call you,' she said in a harsh voice that was unlike her usual smooth efficiency. Kenny had hired Jo-Anne be-cause she was unflappable and not particularly pretty. Today he would not have recognised her.

'He'll turn up,' said Misty, keeping her voice uncon-
cerned. There was always the fear in the back of her
mind that one day he wouldn't, but she could not admit
to that. 'At least we know where he is now—in
Acapulco.'

The telephone rang and Jo-Anne picked it up.
'Turner,' she told Misty quietly, covering the mouth-
piece with her hand.

Misty's heart stopped. 'I'll take it in my office.'

She closed the door and lifted her receiver, then heard
the click of Jo-Anne going off the line. 'Misty Donovan
here. Yes?'

'This is Zeb,' the voice told her. Her heart settled into
a normal beat as the voice said, 'Are we all set for
tonight?'

She should have known last night, when she'd watched
the man across the pool, unable to reconcile her own
impressions... There *were* two men. She pushed a button
to signal Jo-Anne to have the call traced. 'Well, Mr
Turner, I think we should go over one or two things.'

He did not like that. 'What's the problem? It's
straightforward.'

'It's anything but straightforward.' She let her pencil
go. A caricature, but the eyes were right; something not
quite direct in them, the latent awareness of his own
charm. Not one man, but two. She said, 'I need more
details on the marina.'

She asked questions interminably, and he answered,
although she could sense the impatience, hear it in his
voice. She should have known. The impatience was
totally out of character. Zeb Turner was a careful man,
patient and honest.

'Is that it?' he asked finally, just after Jo-Anne slipped
in and dropped a piece of paper on her desk. A tele-

phone number and an address. He was calling from here in San Diego. He said urgently, 'You understand that it's essential you keep to the role, pretend you don't know me at all.'

'Yes, that's it. Goodbye, Mr Turner.'

'Just a minute! Are you——?' She pushed the disconnect button.

'Did you hang up on him?' Jo-Anne was intrigued and a little shocked, her tongue worrying her upper front teeth. Shocking things were always happening around Misty and Kenny Donovan.

'Hmm,' she agreed, wedging the receiver under her chin and flipping through the telephone-book. 'It's good for him. I don't think people do it enough. If he calls again, tell him I'm out for the day, but that everything's fine.'

She had the number she wanted and she was dialling it. It was not the number Jo-Anne had written on the paper.

'Mr Turner, please,' she told the voice that answered, and Jo-Anne blinked in confusion, then she left the room because Misty nodded that she wanted privacy.

'Who's calling please?' the well-trained voice was asking.

She grinned and said, 'Tell him he'd better be impulsive and take this call. It's important.'

'Really! I——'

'I'll wait.' She would be willing to bet that he did not take a lot of chances, but she hoped he would take this one. If not, she would persuade the secretary to put her through, but——

'What's your name?' Lord, she had a built-in detector for the man! Her heart went wild at the sound of his voice, her breathing weak.

'Misty,' she said, and she laughed when he did.

'Misty,' he repeated, as if tasting the flavour of it. 'It would be.'

She smiled at something warm in his voice, admitted, 'Actually, my name is Dawn.'

'I'm glad you called.' His voice was warm, as if she were an old friend he had missed. 'I've been trying to trace you, but I haven't a lot of clues.'

'My licence-plate number?' she suggested. 'The guard must have written it down.' She twisted a curl around her finger. Of course it was unprofessional. Making this call at all was somewhat unethical, but she did not believe she owed anything to a client who had not paid yet, and had not spoken a word of truth.

'I dreamed about you, Misty. Will you have dinner with me?' His voice was strained, as if the invitation were not quite what he had intended. She thought about Alice Vandaniken and knew that Zeb was remembering her too. 'Thursday,' he said, and she wondered what he intended and what he had done with the thought of his mistress.

'No.' Her voice had a huskiness she did not intend. Alice was safe. She did not date. She had decided it was not worth the pain. The only exception was a policeman she knew, and their monthly dinner and dancing date was more for the exchange of mutually useful information than for any romantic purpose.

Silence, as if he were listening to what she did not say. Finally, he spoke, his voice half amused, half curious. 'Why did you call me?' She drew a deep line across the forehead of the caricature doodle in front of her. The two faces, side by side on the page. Two different men, technically identical.

'Do you have a video recorder in your office?'

He laughed then, and she drew in laugh lines. 'No, Misty, I don't. I have one at home. Do—no, just a moment.' He was talking to someone else, quick and low, then to her, 'Misty, I wonder if we'll ever have an ordinary conversation. First last night, then——' He laughed, as if enjoying himself, then said oddly, 'You know, this is one of the busiest days in my year. I don't know why I'm spending part of it talking to a strange pretty girl who wears a sexy blue bathing-suit. Do you want to borrow my video recorder? And how did you know about my union problems?'

She stilled her heart. Blue bathing-suits weren't the issue, nor was his rather unexpected effect on her. 'Is one of your brothers your twin?'

'My——' She heard the noise of his chair jerking erect, then his voice was businesslike and she could feel the stillness of his face. 'Yes. Barry. He's in Paris. He's flying back here tonight. Why?'

'He's not in Paris.' She rattled off a telephone number and said, 'That's where he is. It's not just your union and your nephew that are giving you trouble. I'm sending you a parcel by messenger. Take a look at it before the day's over. It's important.'

'What——?'

'Goodbye,' she said softly. 'And please, watch out for that brother of yours.'

'Just a second! Don't hang up! Misty—Misty who? What's your name? Your address?'

She heard the frustration in his voice as she hung up, and could not help smiling. He was not used to mysteries. She decided that a little curiosity would do him good.

CHAPTER THREE

MAX froze, his legs stiffening in the sand, his pointed nose rigid as his ears twitched. Misty stopped behind him, her bare toes curling in the sand.

'What is it, Max?' There was laughter in her voice. Max was a frustrated watchdog who had little opportunity to practise his profession. She had known him to lose his cool over a paper bag tumbling along the beach in the wind.

He growled, his attention focusing on the house. She looked in the direction he was sending the low, threatening noise. There was nothing. The white walls of her house against the beach. The sand. The water. The only sign of life was the tall, lean forms of palm trees. Max growled, oddly certain that the threat came from the direction of the house. That had to mean someone on the driveway, concealed by the white wall in front of the house.

'Company, Max?' This was her place, private, and since she really did not have a social life, no one came here. The newspaper came to the office, and the electric meter man had come last week. 'Kenny? Is it Kenny, Max?'

The dog growled again. It must be Kenny. She started to run, hurrying because he might not wait for her to answer the door. He would know she was home. Her car was in the driveway in front of the house, yet it wouldn't be unlike Kenny to decide she did not want to answer the door, to turn away and leave.

She had arrived home only twenty minutes ago, changed into shorts and halter-neck top and gone down to the water with Max, sharing the wind and the sound of the surf with the dog, the last moments before the sun set in a red explosion on the western horizon. Now she ran quietly through the sand, padded barefoot across her tiled patio, the dog beside her, keeping pace but moving slowly for his quick legs, as if he did not want her to go.

She heard the buzzer as she crossed the patio, then silence. Max growled again, the sound low and threatening.

'Behave yourself,' she hissed. The dog slunk back, sat down, but his eyes never left that front door. Misty made her voice threatening. 'Shut up, you mongrel, or you won't get another bone for a week!' Calling him a mongrel was the worst insult she could think of. He was pure-bred and temperamental, and he whined as she spoke. Max and Kenny, the two most important beings in her life, disliked each other intensely.

Max was silent, watchful. She opened the door to the house, hurried along the walk to the gate in the wall. Then she paused for a second, stilling her face and sub-duing the relief, the love. When she was sure she had it under control, she turned the knob.

'Hello, stranger. How was Acapulco?' Her voice was casual, a smile greeting as she swung the door open. She heard Max disobeying her with one low growl and she said sharply, 'Max!' before she saw the man.

She should have known it wasn't Kenny. He would turn up in his own time, casually walking into the office at midday as if he had never left. She could count on her fingers the number of times he had come to her home.

'Acapulco's fine, as far as I know.' He smiled slightly, took in her confusion with those hazel eyes. 'I'm sorry to disappoint you,' he said gently.

'What?' She felt crazily flustered, the disappointment of not seeing Kenny quickly replaced by something that could not be panic.

'You were expecting someone else.' Close up, she could see the warm gold tones of his eyes. He was dressed in a subdued suit. She thought he must have just come from his office, and that he had been sitting too long, bent over papers and books.

She did not know what to say to him, had not expected him to find her at all. 'Did you get the tape I sent?' She knew he had. The courier had confirmed delivery.

He nodded, smiling, 'Do you ever take part in ordinary conversations? Like "Hello, Zeb. How are you?"'

She grinned, remembering how she had confronted him in the whirlpool the night before. 'It's you,' she explained lightly. 'I keep expecting you to be someone else.'

'Can I come in?' He saw her stiffen, and saw his eyes change from warm gold to hazel as he asked, 'Who's in Acapulco?'

'I——' She blinked. 'I thought you were someone else.'

'You said that.' Of course she had. She felt stupid, awkward, and she was not accustomed to feeling that way.

He asked again, 'Can I come in? Please, Misty. I can't talk to anyone else about this. Only you.'

She should have been able to refuse him, to insist that they go somewhere else to talk. Her office. A restaurant. Not here. Somehow, though, it was impossible to refuse him. She stepped back and he was inside the screen door, then inside her door. He closed both doors behind himself, then stilled as the dog growled. The dog was very quiet, his eyes locked with the man's.

It was strange, but Max was looking his most threatening, yet this man was not frightened. Wary, yes, but she could see his eyes and he was not even thinking of diving back through her front door.

'Most people panic when Max growls.'

He stretched out his arm slightly, fingers hanging down slackly, an offering to the dog. 'That would be foolish, wouldn't it? He was warning me, not threatening.' It was a subtle distinction, and one most people did not make.

Max stood up and moved closer without seeming to move his legs. His nose twitched, but he did not come within reach of Zeb's hand. 'He doesn't trust men,' Misty explained.

He said quietly, 'Perhaps that's because you don't trust them either.'

She swallowed. He was much more dangerous than his brother, and she had been insane to send him that tape, to warn him about his nephew and the union problems. He did not need anyone to help him keep control of his life. He was standing there, unafraid of Max and looking right through her into her private place, at the fears and insecurities that had nothing to do with him or his business in coming here.

'You're dressed this time,' she said lightly, changing the subject and hoping to disconcert him, but he only smiled as his eyes fixed on her, taking everything in.

He said, 'But you're not.' She glanced down at her bare legs, bare feet, the skimpy halter-neck top. He said whimsically, 'If I hadn't seen that tape, I'd think you never wear clothes.'

His words seemed to undress her and she had a sudden unnerving fantasy of herself standing in front of him bare and naked, every inch of her body exposed and held there in his gaze. She saw him lick his lips, and when he cleared his throat she knew that he had seen her fantasy.

And that he wanted her.

Had she been insane, inviting him inside her home? She had taken judo and used it more than once, but she did not fool herself that he would be an easy opponent. He—no, he was not the kind of man who took without asking. He was civilised, conventional, and it had been her weird mind creating those fantasies.

He moved, two steps further into her home. Max was still, watching, not exactly relaxing, but accepting this stranger's presence in his home. Misty found herself following Zeb, being led through her own home. 'Out here, I think,' he said when he found the patio. He turned back and his eyes flowed over her bare legs again, up to her brief shorts, coming to rest finally on the swelling of her breasts under the top. 'It's getting cool, though, now that the sun's gone down. Do you want to get changed into something warmer? I'll wait here for you.'

She realised then that she was shivering, standing here in bare feet, staring at him. She was not actually cold, but she said, 'Yes, I will.' She walked away from him, then looked back. He looked tired. She thought about the union business, about the tape she had sent him. 'Would you like something to drink?' she asked.

'Yes. Thanks.' He smiled at her, and the tiredness was hidden now. 'Scotch,' he suggested.

She shook her head. 'Sorry, not my style. Coke? Ginger ale? Lemonade? Any of those. Coffee? No, not coffee. I suspect you've had too much coffee already today.'

'You'd be right. I'll try the ginger ale.'

She brought it back to him, finding him leaning back in the lounge chair, looking out at the beach and the water. He smiled at her, accepting the glass without a word. She found herself smiling back, then was in her bedroom before she realised how odd that little contact had been. The glass. The smiles. Zeb leaning back in the lounge chair looking at her beach, her water, as if it was his. The strange easiness of their not speaking, just smiling as if they were together always and knew each other too well to need the words.

She wished she could make up her mind whether to feel uneasy or comfortable with this man. She grinned at her own image in her mirror, laughing at herself. He's nothing. A not-quite-client. A man you'll never see again.

Her image was not convinced. Conventional, she reminded herself. Like Wayne. Her reflection blinked at her, and the sense of dreaminess was gone. She and Zeb Turner were worlds apart, and she knew only too well how much distance separated those worlds.

She put on jeans and a big, loose-knit sweater. Normally she went barefoot at home, but she dug through her wardrobe and found a pair of sandals. She checked herself in the mirror before she went back to him. She was very well-covered, almost shapeless under the sweater. Her blonde hair was tumbled everywhere in a wild chaos that looked vaguely sensuous. She picked up her brush and brushed it hard. Then she found herself putting on lipstick, and she stopped that. Make-up only made her look more like a fluffy blonde. She scrubbed the colour off and found she looked pale, too pale.

The hell with him! Why had he come here?

She found him where he had been when she left, lying back motionless in the lounge chair. He didn't look back to see her when she came into the patio, but he knew she was there. 'Do you want this chair?' he asked in a lazy voice.

'No, thanks.' She crossed to the edge of the patio. She set her glass of Coke on the ledge, then lifted herself up and sat there leaning against the pillar, cross-legged, looking down at him and feeling the sand and the sea behind her. A lot of men would have felt uncomfortable with her there, above them, watching. He didn't.

'I like your home, Misty Dawn,' he said finally, his voice easy and warm, as if he had known her forever. 'I don't think I've ever been in a place I like so much.'

'It's small.' It was, but the size had never bothered her. There was only her and Max, and the beach stretched on forever. Of course, there were other houses nearby, other people who could use that beach, but she was the only one who seemed to like walking the sand in the evenings when it was not summertime. She had never figured that out, why most Californians stayed away from the beach after September came.

He was very quiet, and she had a strange feeling that he might lie there forever, just soaking in the ocean. She found herself asking. 'Why do you call me Misty Dawn?'

He smiled. She liked the way the lines deepened around his lips, as if he smiled that quiet smile a lot. His brother's smile was different, more mischievous perhaps, and not as sincere. She saw him shrug, and saw only a hint of the hard muscles she knew were under the suit jacket. He had undone the buttons of his jacket and she could see the pale brown shirt moving as he breathed.

'I don't know,' he said, and it took her a second to remember what her question had been. 'You said your name was Dawn, and it was an appealing image.' He said that self-consciously, as if his fanciful thought made him a little uncomfortable.

'My dad used to call me that. Then after a while everyone started calling me Misty.' She had never told anyone else about that. Not even Wayne, strangely enough.

'Used to?' It was a question, asked gently, as if he knew this was a place that hurt.

'He——' How could she answer when she did not know the details herself? 'Long past,' she said with a shake of her head that sent the curls back into disarray. 'I hope you didn't mind my leaving Max here when I went to change. He can be alarming.'

Zeb grinned, his eyes going to the dog. Max had relaxed enough to lie down, but his eyes were still watching Zeb. 'He just kept an eye on me, made sure I didn't steal the silver.'

'There's no silver here.' His girlfriend, Alice, would have silver, and a very elegant apartment in the penthouse of that big building she owned. 'You said you had to talk to me?' She wondered why he and Alice had not married after all those years of their high-class affair. He was turning his empty glass in his hand and she opened her lips to offer him another drink, but the words stayed inside. It would be better not to draw out his time here. She had begun to think she would have to ask him again, that he would not speak, when he finally said quietly, 'I've got a problem. I need your help.'

She looked down at him, unable to resist a slight smile. His world was very organised, except for the troublemaking brother. She was curious to know the story behind the crazy kidnapping idea, and she suspected that he might tell her now if she asked. Still, she felt a cautious nervousness and she said, 'You have a lot problems. You're good at solving them. Why would you need my help?'

'Well . . .' He looked around at the patio. She could see him taking in the slight disorder: her bathing-suit hanging over the lawn chair, the remains of Max's bone on the edge of the tile floor. She wasn't sure what he was thinking, but he smiled a little and she suppressed the urge to scramble up and pick up the bone, put away the bathing-suit, as he said, 'Today, Misty Dawn, I'm in a little over my head.'

'Are you?' She grinned. 'Last night you were swimming over your head, but it was a very civilised pool and you were in no danger. You're a good swimmer.'

He grimaced, half a smile and half discomfort. 'Why do you look at me like that?'

'Like what?' Her smile died and she felt her heart pounding. It was crazy, but she was suddenly frightened. Not physically intimidated, but something else, like a premonition.

'As if you're going to laugh. As if I'm amusing you.' He grinned, admitted, 'I'm not used to that,' and her nervousness seemed to flow away like a smooth river.

'I'll bet you're not.' She giggled, spreading her hands in an expressive gesture that took in Zeb as he lay comfortably relaxed on her lounger. It struck her suddenly how impossible it was that he should be here in her home, looking as if he belonged. 'Last night, when I confronted you in that pool, you looked like someone who'd wandered into another world. And today, at my

door, you were half afraid to come in. Do you think I'm
dangerous?'

'Very.' But he was smiling, then suddenly not smiling
as he said carefully, 'But I'm going to take the chance.
I think it'll be worth it.' She was not quite sure what he
meant, and somehow she was afraid to ask. He said, 'I
need you to advise me about Barry.'

'Your twin brother.' She grasped at the change of
subject. This was easier, business, and the questions came
automatically. 'Have you any idea why he wanted to pull
that stunt on you? It was a stunt, wasn't it? You weren't
in on it?'

'No, of course not, but I'll admit that I almost wish
you'd done it. It would have been quite an interesting
experience.'

'Interesting! Interesting? I——' Kidnapping Zeb? His
twin's idea had been insane, a crazy plot. Knock-out
drops and—if she were doing it, she would use Max, she
supposed, yet somehow she was not sure if Max would
stop this man from escaping.

'What are you thinking, Misty Dawn?'

The cottage in Mexico. Across the border in a
speedboat. It would be illegal entry, of course, but why
pause at that when it was kidnapping anyway? Zeb, re-
gaining consciousness, lying on the bed in the cabin.
Waking up her prisoner. Herself——

His voice penetrated finally. 'Hey, what's wrong?'

She twisted her face away from him quickly, looking
out over the water. What a wild, oddly erotic fantasy!
She licked her lips and hoped her face had not shown
what she was feeling inside. Unsettling. Weird.

'Nothing,' she said raggedly. 'I was just thinking
about—nothing. I sent you the tape. That's all the am-

munition you need. Surely whatever he's trying to do, you can confront him and——'

He stood up and she lost track of her words. He had seemed to be planted in that lounge chair forever, but suddenly he was on his feet and far too close. He was standing near, in front of her, and she could not get down and away from him without coming even closer. She made herself very still and told herself that he was a very dull man. Conventional. Stodgy. The kind of upper-class bore that turned her off.

Her heart was pounding and she felt as if she would explode from holding herself still and hiding the wild, unidentified emotions. He was very close and she did not understand why he affected her this way. He was frowning, and she wished she were able to help, to smooth away the tension that held the lines of his face. Even as she had the thought, she knew that she was exactly the opposite of what a man like this would want in a woman or a friend.

The dark was growing now and they were surrounded with stillness that wrapped them in an intimate silence. He said thoughtfully, 'Do I make you nervous?' He didn't make her answer that, but stepped back. 'Misty, I didn't want to confront him. Not if I can help it. With Barry, that's not usually the best way.'

She could face him then. It was getting too dark to see his eyes, to see the gold and the hazel, but his voice was busy with working out a strategy. 'Is that what you do?' she asked, knowing the answer. 'Handle them all? Tactfully? Without confrontations?'

'If I can. Yes. Why not?' He stepped back to her, but this time she was able to keep still inside until his fingers touched a curl on her cheek, lightly brushed it back before he realised he was touching her and pulled his hand back. 'How would you do it?'

'Differently.' She shook her head. 'I don't think we live in the same world.' He nodded, and somehow his agreement made her feel very lonely. When he paced back across the patio, away from her, she slipped down and bent to pick up Max's bone.

'How did you know it was me?' His voice sounded odd against the evening breeze that rustled the palm trees behind her. 'When I called you, and now at your door, you knew it was me and not Barry. How?' She shrugged his question away, but he seemed very intent, very determined. 'Most people can't tell us apart.'

'You've got to be joking!'

'We're identical twins, Misty Dawn.' Why did she not stop him calling her that?

'Of course you are,' she agreed. 'That's obvious. But only a fool would mix you up after meeting you both.' The same hair, the same bones under the tanned flesh, but the men could not be farther apart.

He did not understand, and she could see that it worried at him and he had to know. He said, 'I saw that tape. Barry was dressed like me, acting like me. Why is that funny?' He swung on her, and she was not sure if it was anger in his eyes or not. 'You were doodling, drawing what looked like his face—my face.'

'No,' she insisted, suddenly not laughing any more. 'Not yours. He was dressed like you, but—he couldn't play you in a million years.' They were such different men, the one with the feel of a con artist, and this one with the feel of an old friend, someone you trusted in the darkest moments, someone exciting and...

'Even my mother can be confused which one of us she's talking to.'

'Then your mother's a fool!' she said angrily. He was not convinced, and suddenly it seemed very important to her. 'Just a minute. Wait. I'll show you.'

She slipped down, ran into her bedroom and found her bag where she had tossed it on her bed. She didn't know why she had put the paper from her desk into her bag, but it was there, two men sketched side by side. She brought it to him. He was waiting—the man had an incredible talent for staying still, although she could feel the life flowing in him. 'That's Barry,' she said, handing it to him and pointing. 'I'm no artist, but——'

'It's Barry,' he agreed, taking it from her hands, his voice alert as if he was seeing something he had not seen before.

She pointed to the other face, said, 'You should be able to see the difference.'

She watched him, suddenly self-conscious. He stared at both pictures and he could not have missed the difference. They were caricatures, not accurate sketches. She had put down her impression of the two men, and the drawings showed emotions and feelings more than features. She realised too late that what he was seeing was her own reactions to both men. When he looked up, she said quickly, defensively, 'It was bothering me. I knew last night something didn't make sense; *you* just didn't add up. If I had known you were twins——'

He grinned at that, said, 'I'm not twins. I have a twin.'

'If I'd known that, I'd have guessed as soon as I— there's not much similar between you two, except for looks. You're under control and he's restless. Your eyes are more hazel and gold. His are green. And he hasn't got around to growing up yet. You grew up a long time ago.'

'Because I was the older.' He shifted, and she thought she could see the weight that had been on him for years, all those people leaning on him, his mother and his mistress and perhaps his brother as well—certainly his brother's ex-wife and son. 'I was ten minutes older, but somehow that always put me in the position of being responsible.'

'And you never fought it?'

'No,' he agreed quietly, accepting his responsibilities the way she supposed he always did. 'Would you have fought it?' he asked.

'I don't know. I don't have family.' His eyes narrowed and she added quickly, 'Not like that,' because of course she had Kenny. 'How did you find me?'

He laughed then for the first time, and she liked the sound of his laughter; it was low-pitched and sounded as if it surprised him. His laughter deepened the light lines of his face, making him look both older and younger at the same time. He said, 'Maybe you should hire me. I played private detective, and I can't be too bad at it, because I found you. First I tried the docket on that tape.' He grimaced, and she knew that he had learned nothing there. She and Kenny used that courier regularly, and the docket would not have listed Donovan and Donovan or an address.

'Then what? My licence-plates?' That must have been it. She had made the suggestion herself last night, and he had got her plates from the guard.

He walked across the patio, back to where she had resumed her perch on the ledge. She saw him slip the two pictures into his pocket and opened her lips to protest, but there was no reason why he should not have them. They were only doodles.

'I tried your idea about the plates.' His slipped his hands into the pockets of his trousers. She had an odd feeling that he was trapping them, so that he would not reach out again to caress her hair. 'The guard wasn't nearly as efficient as you imagined. He thought you were——' He cleared his throat, then continued '—thought you were meeting me, so he didn't do any of the things he should have done. Didn't get a look at your pass——'

'I didn't have one, and he thought that because I let him think that.' She saw his brows lift and said quickly, 'I was working, and it—well, it's an easy way to get past a guard. Nobody suspects fluffy-looking blonde women of anything.'

'Fluffy?' He laughed, his voice booming out, and one hand came out and touched the side of her face. She would have jerked away, but the pillar was there, right behind her, and there was nowhere to go. 'Misty Dawn, you're far too perceptive and intelligent to be described as fluffy by anyone.'

She swallowed, and his fingers seemed to take forever to slide away from her cheek. She swallowed again and licked her lips, and was not sure if her voice would work at all. 'So how did you find me?'

'An old schoolfriend.' She blinked and he smiled. She had to smile back when she realised that he felt quite proud of managing to track her. 'We were seniors together, shared a rather wild graduation party, and haven't seen each other more than five times since then. But I thought of him this afternoon when I was trying to think of how to find you.'

'Why?' She knew she was encouraging him, but she wanted to see him enjoying a bit of sleuthing, and she wanted to know how he had found this place.

'He's on the police force, and it was obvious from the tape that you were a private detective. I thought he might know who you were, or how I could find out. There can't be that many private detectives in San Diego who look like you.'

'So you found the office. But how did you find me out here?' That was a little unnerving. Not all of her clients were the kind of people she would want to find her home. That was why her telephone was unlisted and her name not on the gate outside.

He was still very close. In the light from the house she could see the faint shadow of his beard under the skin of his chin. 'My friend,' he explained. He pushed back the hair from his forehead, although it had been smoothly brushed and orderly. 'He said that he thought you had a place out on the beach in the Mission Bay area. So I came for a drive, looking for a white Corvette.'

She smiled. 'Not bad, actually. Don't tell me this is the only white Corvette out here?'

'No. There's one three miles that way.' He gestured and she smiled when he grimaced. 'It's owner is six foot four and was quite suspicious of my motives. For a minute I was afraid he belonged to you, then his wife turned up.'

She grinned, imagining him trying to explain. But he would have managed somehow, smoothly. 'You haven't told me what your twin brother was up to.'

'I'll tell you now. Then I'd like you to go ahead and kidnap me.'

CHAPTER FOUR

'BUT why?' She had jumped down from her perch long ago, had paced the patio and listened to Zeb's explanation. The light was gone now. A few moments ago Zeb had walked over and lit the small gas lantern that stood in the corner of the patio.

Now he explained, 'Barry's always short of cash, and he's always pushing for us to declare more dividends.'

'I don't mean that,' she said impatiently. 'I understand what you've told me.' She ticked off items on her fingers, her slight body a dark silhouette against the moonlit sky. 'You and Neil want the capital for expansion in Mexico. Barry, your twin, wants the cash instead, dividends issued and to hell with capital expansion. Your mother always votes with Barry. But——' her voice emphasised the next words '——you and Neil swing the majority of the voting stock, so Barry would be outvoted at the meeting tomorrow.'

'If Helen votes with us,' he corrected, and he wondered at himself confiding so many family secrets in this woman; yet he knew that she would be worthy of his trust.

'Helen? Your brother's ex-wife? She wouldn't vote with Barry?'

'Not normally, but if Barry thinks his kidnapping scheme has failed, there's no telling what he might try. I'd like to keep him happy until that meeting, avoid his dreaming up some other wild scheme.'

'Or finding someone who actually will kidnap you? Would he actually try to pretend he was you at the meeting?' Zeb nodded and she said, 'Surely he couldn't get away with that? Not in a meeting with your own family. Your mother and your other brother.'

'He might get away with it.' He frowned at her, admitted, 'My mother's nowhere near as observant as you are. Neil—well, Neil might pick up something, but on the other hand he might not be in a very observant frame of mind tomorrow. He's flying in from Canada early tomorrow morning, and he's probably thinking more about the woman he's leaving back there than about meetings or business. He might not notice. If I'm not there at home tonight, Keith might worry and stay up to tell his dad when he gets in. And they'd all be relieved when I turned up at the meeting, after thinking I'd gone missing.'

'No!' She bit her lip, worried because she did not want to believe his family could fall for this. 'Barry wanted me to call your place, to leave a message that you wouldn't be home tonight, but you'd see Neil at the meeting.'

He frowned. 'No reason? No explanation? I wouldn't do that. There's my nephew there, and he'd be expecting me home, and Neil expecting me to be there when he arrives.'

'Uncharacteristic behaviour,' she agreed, 'But if a call like that came, do you really think they'd worry? They'd *wonder*, of course, but wouldn't they accept it and ask questions later?'

He swung around, staring at her. 'Yes, they'd accept it. Why not? After all, they'd never think I was kidnapped. Why would they?' He laughed and admitted, 'None of this is my usual style, all this drama. Kidnapping. Conspiracies. Mysterious blonde women. They would never dream of that.'

'Yet you're getting involved in the conspiracy. Why?'

'Let's walk,' he suggested. He was relieved when she came to his side, going with him down the steps along the sandy beach. He wanted to reach out and catch her hand, but he knew that if he did she would jerk back and that strangely warm communication between them would disappear. She was, as he had said, a mysterious woman, and he had this crazy, insane need to keep her close to him, to find out why her eyes were shadowed and to learn what made her laugh and what her eyes looked like when they were filled with passion.

Of course, he wanted to deal with Barry, too, and there was some truth in what he said now, as they walked along the sand. 'Barry's been doing far too much of this,' he said slowly. 'Not kidnapping attempts, but trying to manipulate me, and the games get dirtier. I'd like to teach him a bit of a lesson, but on the other hand I don't want open warfare. If he gets angry, he can react recklessly, and I wouldn't like him to try to get back at me by doing something to hurt Helen or Julian.'

'Why would he do that?' She stopped, turning to stare at him. She had taken her sandals off, going barefoot in the sand with the sandals swinging from her hand— the same hand that was closest to him, the one he had been wanting to take into his grasp. 'How could he hit you through your sister-in-law? Are you in love with her?'

He frowned. 'No.' The question somehow brought Alice to his mind. Not that he loved Alice, but he cared about her. He wondered suddenly what he was doing here, why he wanted to be walking in the sand with this woman when he knew nothing of her except that she stirred his hormones and she was different, very different, from anyone he had met before.

'But she's in your care,' said Misty thoughtfully. 'And perhaps Barry knows you quite well. So what is it that you want to do? What do you want me to do?' She laughed then, and he could hear real pleasure in her voice, as if she had thought of something exciting and fun. 'I wonder if this is unethical, my plotting with you. After all, we're plotting against my client.'

'Are we?' The smile in her voice made him feel light-hearted. He was ridiculously glad that Barry had brought her into his life. 'I'm Zeb Turner. Wasn't that the name of your client?' He liked her laughter, light and warm. 'Are you going to co-operate with me?' he asked, laughing himself because his words sounded like something out of a B-movie.

'Yes, all right, but I think you've got to do more than just disappear for the night. I'll make the call, just as Barry suggested. Then I think if you really want to defuse him, you should turn up at that meeting with me on your arm.'

'Playing the part of my fancy piece?'

'No!' Her sandals slapped against her jeans and she swallowed. Yes, that was what she had meant. It was the kind of play-acting that went with her profession, but she had never played that kind of game with anyone but Kenny. It had never been anything more than a mask they wore. He said something, and she said, 'What?'

'It's a good idea. Would you really do that for me?' His voice was serious now, and she knew what he would be like in a business meeting, thoughtful yet decisive. 'I like it. You at the meeting with me. We won't say a word, but it will keep Barry off balance.' He laughed again then, and the businessman was gone. 'Just for once,

Barry will have to stick to business for a whole meeting. He wouldn't dare do anything else for fear I'll expose his little plot.' The businessman returned and Zeb said briskly, 'I'll pay your fee, of course.'

She stopped herself from refusing to take the money. It was better that way. She would charge him for it, then their relationship would lose that strange significance it seemed to have.

'I guess I'd better stay here tonight,' he said lightly.

'What?' She stopped walking. Him? Here? In her house? 'What are you talking about?'

'I'm supposed to be kidnapped,' he reminded her. He had walked two steps past her, then stopped and looked back at her standing alone with the dog at her side. He wondered again who the man was that she had thought she was opening the door for. She wore no rings, but there was a man in Acapulco.

'But you're not actually being kidnapped.' Her voice had cooled and was brisk, the voice she had used with Barry in that tape he had viewed. 'There's absolutely no need for you to spend the night here.'

'I can't go home, though, can I?' He wanted to stay. It was an ache inside him that no one but her could satisfy. 'If I go to a hotel, I'm likely to be seen.'

'Only if you go to the kind of a hotel your friends and family would frequent.' She turned away, reached out for her dog. Her voice was muffled. 'Take your car and go to a budget motel on the highway somewhere. No one will ever know. I'll meet you tomorrow. You can come to my office and——'

'But Barry might go there,' he said reasonably. 'It would be much simpler if I stayed here. I could sleep on your sofa, and there would be no need for me to meet you anywhere. We could go straight to the meeting in the morning.'

She was very still, knowing she had to get him out of here, that she could not possibly sleep with him on her sofa. It was impossible, yet she was a little uncertain that he would simply *go* when she asked. 'No,' she said, but her voice was not as cool as it should have been.

'Why not? Would the man in Acapulco object?'

'No,' she said slowly, the words coming without permission. 'He wouldn't care.'

'He's crazy, then,' Zeb Turner said softly. 'If I'd been the man you were waiting for tonight, I'd care like hell if you let another man sleep under your roof.'

She shook her head, confused and bewildered by her own feelings, angry with herself for losing her cool. 'Will you make the call, then?' he asked, speaking as if he'd had to say it more than once to get her attention. She nodded and he said, 'Good. Call right away, would you? I don't want my nephew to be worried about my not getting home for dinner.' He stared at her, not coming any closer, although she felt as if he were pressing against her space, a strangely gentle threat. 'I'll pick you up in the morning. Seven-thirty. All right?'

She nodded, uncertain of why he had suddenly dropped the suggestion that he sleep on her sofa. Had it been a joke, a teasing suggestion that he had never intended to follow through on? Had she really felt herself weakening, getting ready to let him lie on her living-room sofa while she tried to sleep in her own bed only feet away?

'Where are you going?' she asked breathlessly. He shrugged and she thought suddenly that he would go to Alice. 'You can stay here,' she said, gasping as she heard her own words.

He stepped up to her and Max growled. 'No, Misty Dawn. I don't think you really mean that.' Max's back stiffened and Zeb said thoughtfully, 'Now, I wonder why he thinks I'm a threat now.'

'He's neurotic.' She jerked in a ragged breath and wondered where her sanity had gone. 'He barks at paper bags and chases waves. He only looks like a guard dog. He's effective because people are afraid of Dobermanns, but really he's a quivering coward. Maybe he growled at you, but more likely he thought he heard something.'

'I don't think so.' Zeb's hands came up and cupped her face, gently, as if afraid of frightening her. 'I think he knew that I wanted to kiss you.'

She shook her head, but his hands were still there, touching and making her feel terribly vulnerable. Was he really going to kiss her? Was she going to stand here, staring up and him and *letting* him bring his lips to hers, take the trembling craziness that was roaring in her bloodstream and taste it?

'Alice,' she said desperately, throwing the name between them. 'Your mistress. You can't—I'm not—you're not the kind of man who plays around, and she——' She gulped and wondered what the hell she was talking about, wondered when she would get her normal self back.

Yet he nodded as if she were making perfect sense. 'Yes, I know.' She had no idea just *what* he was agreeing to, but his thumbs were rubbing gently along the sides of her neck. She knew that he felt it when she swallowed, and she was afraid he could feel the trembling inside her. 'I'll have to do something about Alice,' he said slowly.

She stared at him. He was far too tall for her. He lived a life like the one Wayne had lived, and yet—no! He was—this was insane. She knew how ridiculously insane it was.

'What about the man in Acapulco?' he asked, then he was very still, even his thumbs stilled, as he waited for her to answer.

'What about him?' she managed. He thought she had a lover, a man in Acapulco. 'What are you asking?' She swallowed, and that lump in her throat had turned into a permanent fixture. 'I don't think you—you want me to dump my—my lover?'

He laughed, said softly, 'Yes, I suppose that is what I want. Misty Dawn, you don't dress things up, do you?'

'No.' She shivered, said, 'Tomorrow you'll wake up and you'll realise that you don't know anything about me, that this is insanity.'

'I don't think so.' He could have been discussing a minor technicality in a business contract. 'I think it's an adventure. You know, when you turned up in that pool, I'd been sitting there wishing something unusual would happen in my life, something new and——'

'Not me!' She kept her voice very sharp. 'If you want a little fling, it's not me.' That wasn't right. She knew he wasn't that kind of man, and the way he'd talked about doing something about Alice, as if he meant this seriously—no, that was impossible! This business with Barry had thrown him more than it appeared. She said dully, 'You really don't know what you're saying. I live in another world, Mr Turner. I play detective games for a living, and I don't have any background at all. I don't know how to be a hostess, and I can't talk cooking and exotic dinner dishes. I don't know my wines and I don't know who my ancestors were. I hate parties, and I——' Oh, lord! Why had she said all that? As if she—as if he——

'Easy, Misty Dawn.' His thumbs were moving again, caressing the tension away from her neck. 'I won't rush you. Maybe this is a crazy insanity I'm feeling, but...' His lips were suddenly there, brushing her open mouth, leaving her tingling and trembling. 'I don't think so,' he whispered. 'But we'll find out, won't we? Tomorrow... and the next day...and the next.'

'No.' Her voice was supposed to be strong, but the protest escaped raggedly, an unconvincing croak. She cleared her throat and felt his hands press gently as her neck muscles tensed against them. 'Let me go!'

His hands dropped away at once, and she wondered why she had not asked him to release her sooner. Max pressed against her and made a dissatisfied noise now in his throat. 'Some watchdog,' she muttered. 'Zeb, I— it's time for you to go. I'll make that phone call. That's easy, and it won't commit you to anything.' He said nothing, and she talked quickly, trying to cover her shuddering confusion. 'You—later you can always go home if you want and forget the whole thing. If—if I don't see you at seven-thirty in the morning, I'll go to work and assume this was all a crazy fantasy.'

He was waiting, not speaking, watching her. She found herself saying some of the things in her mind, words tumbling out with a desperate intensity. 'I don't get involved with clients. I don't let people come here. This is my place, and you—we—this——' She blinked, but he would not go away, and his words about doing something about Alice seemed to be burning into her brain. She felt, again, his intention to move closer. He was going to touch her again. 'This isn't real!' she gasped. 'This isn't the way you behave. Or me. Go away and get some sleep.' She gulped, hearing her own panic. 'Go away. It'll be gone in the morning.'

He stepped back and she could feel herself breathing again. 'I'm going,' he promised. 'Don't panic, Misty Dawn. Or Max,' he added with a laugh, as Max remembered to growl again.

She stood still and watched him, but he stopped when he came abreast of the dog. He crouched down beside Max and offered his hand again. Max stiffened, and she remembered the hours she had spent with Max the day he had come here. Sitting there, talking to him, offering her hand and waiting for him to make up his mind.

'Have a sniff,' Zeb offered the dog now. Max leaned forward a little, his nose twitching. 'Get used to the smell,' Zeb said casually. 'You're going to see more of me.'

This was her place, and he was the invader, but when he walked across her patio and into her house she did not follow. He would go through and out, and then he would be gone. There were no more words to be said between them. If she saw him again, it would be somewhere else, somewhere she had her public mask on, not here, her home where she had no defences, no pretences for outsiders.

It seemed a long time before she heard the muted roar of his engine. She remembered his car well from the two days she had spent following him. It was dark and quiet and conservative, not like her flashy white Corvette. She walked slowly into the house, leaving her sandals on the patio and closing the sliding patio door as she went in. Max dodged inside the door just before she closed it, and she bent to lock it.

'You're some watchdog!' She looked at him, standing there, his shortened black tail twitching as he looked up at her. 'You're supposed to protect me. Instead, you damned near licked his hand!'

Max's tail jerked faster and she laughed. 'Yeah, I know. He's a strange one, isn't he? Hard to shut out.'

He'd been having a bit of a fantasy tonight, thinking he wanted her. It was out of character and he would wake up in the morning feeling uncomfortable and probably nervous that she might take advantage. She wouldn't. She had learned long ago not to let anyone have the chance to push her away. But she would make the telephone call. It would not do any harm, and she had promised.

She pulled out the telephone book from under the telephone-table, and found that the Turner residence was not listed. The marina office was listed, and now, at night, the number might ring through into the guard-house. Even so, she doubted if she could persuade the guard to give her Zeb's home telephone number.

She sat down by the little table. Her stomach was complaining that she had neglected it, talking and walking with Zeb instead of eating, but she was suppressing a yawn at the same time. She reached for her little book, intending to call a contact who could get the unlisted number. Her hand stilled as it touched the red-bound book. She knew that she had not left it open like that. She never did. She always closed it and put it there, under the ledge. She pulled it slowly towards her, and she wasn't at all surprised to find that it was open at the letter T. There was her hairdresser's phone number, and below it was his name in black ink. He must have used his own pen. A fountain pen, she thought. It had a broad nib, or he pushed too hard. He had written his name in full and she smiled a little. Zebediah. She'd be willing to bet that no one ever called him that, and that he wished his mother had never thought of it. His middle name was John, and she wondered why he didn't use it, except she realised at once that he wasn't the kind of a man who dodged the issue like that. All right, Zeb, she thought with a smile, and she didn't know if his getting into her address book amused or frightened her.

It was not the boy that answered, but the man. Neil, he said. He must have come on an earlier flight, and he sounded slightly worried, but not panicked, by Zeb's disappearance. 'Is he all right?' The voice was insistent, and she decided that Barry would not have fooled this man at the meeting.

'He's fine.' She decided not to play games, not to try playing a part and fooling him. She simply said, 'He wanted me to tell you that he'll meet you at the AGM tomorrow morning. He's sorry about the plane, but something urgent came up.'

'Urgent——?'

'It's under control, he said,' she broke in quickly. 'But he can't get free before the meeting. He'll see you there.'

'Who is this?'

'Miss Don——' She stopped herself, deciding it might not be that wise to give her name. Not with Barry trying his pranks. 'I'm Mr Turner's new confidential assistant, and I'm sorry, Mr Turner, but I must go now.'

She went to bed without her supper and slept poorly. She dreamed that Kenny was laughing at her, waving the key at her. He had her parents locked up behind heavy bars, and he would not let them go unless she kidnapped Zeb Turner. She cried, tears burning holes as they crawled down her cheeks, and Kenny only laughed. Then he started ringing the bell and an army appeared, their guns trained on the couple behind the bars. The ringing went on and on and she was ready to scream, to beg, and then——

She fought a tangle of sheets and blankets, twisting and spinning as her hand reached out. Telephone. She pulled it under the covers, silencing the ring, coming awake with a shock.

'Kenny? Kenny, are you all right?' Her voice was hoarse, and the line was silent. Oh, lord! What had he got into this time? The last time, six months ago, he'd ended up in hospital and she had thought he might die. 'Kenny?'

'It's not Kenny. It's me.' She knew who as soon as the voice came, and a sick relief came with it. Kenny would not call at this time of the night unless it was something terrible. But *where* was her damned irresponsible uncle? What if he never came back this time? What if he simply disappeared, as her parents had, and she never saw him again, never knew——

'Misty? Honey, what's wrong?'

His voice calmed her and she whispered, 'Nothing. Nothing. I—I was having a dream.'

'A nightmare?' His voice was soothing, compelling. 'Take a deep breath, Misty, and look out of your window. The sun's up, and it's a beautiful day.'

She followed his instructions, as if she had no will of her own. The sun was shining through her sheer curtains, and she could see bright blue. 'What time is it?'

'Seven.' His voice was matter-of-fact, casual, as if he often telephoned women who screamed another man's name into the receiver. 'Time you woke up, I think.'

'I—yes. My alarm——' It had rung in her dream, the bell that Kenny had sounded. The alarm, and then the telephone. 'Where are you, Zeb? Are you at Alice's?'

'No. I'm in a motel, just the type you suggested.' His voice was faintly irritated as he said, 'And they didn't give me my wake-up call on time, so I'm calling to make sure you don't think I'm not coming. I'm going to be a couple of minutes late. I just have to shave and shower, then I'll be there. Will you wait?'

So he had not changed his mind, and Barry Turner was going to have a very uncomfortable morning. She smiled, imagining how the brother would feel when Zeb walked in with her on his arm. 'Yes,' she agreed. 'I'll wait. I'll be late anyway, because I've slept in, too.'

'OK.' He sounded very alert for a man who had just woken up. 'Shall we say quarter to eight?'

'Yes,' she agreed, finding the pencil in her hand, another sketch of Zeb appearing on the pad of paper on her bedside-table. 'We'll say a quarter to eight.'

'Good. We'll go to the meeting, then after that we'll have lunch together and you'll explain to me just where Kenny fits into your life, and Acapulco, and why you're having such nightmares about it.'

No, she would not. The meeting, yes, and the game he wanted to play with Barry. But nothing more. She might let him buy her lunch, because she would not be able to bring herself to take money from him for this crazy caper, but there was no way they would talk about Misty Donovan's private life.

She showered, practising how she would keep him at a distance. Then she dressed, careful to wear a business-like suit, one that made her feel like the woman she was, confident and independent, and not about to get involved in an affair with another man like Wayne. Or any man, for that matter. She put her lipstick on, and some mascara, and told herself sternly to remember how good the last few years had been, and how miserable that year with Wayne.

By the time Zeb Turner rang her doorbell, she was able to walk briskly to the door and step outside without letting him in. 'We'd better take my car,' she announced in businesslike tones. 'It would put Barry on guard if your car drove up.' She was careful not to look directly at him. She opened her passenger door for him and got into the driver's seat herself, then she could concentrate on driving without it being obvious that she was avoiding his eyes.

She was on the San Diego freeway before he spoke to her. She had turned on to number five a couple of minutes ago, changed lanes into the left lane. Now she was driving, fast and smooth in the fast lane, the traffic very orderly around her. She settled back in her seat and relaxed a little. She liked driving fast. The car did it well, and she was a skilled driver. Once she had dated a racing-car driver and he had given her some tips, and she had listened because she liked speed, but wanted to minimise the dangers.

'I find this very exciting,' Zeb's voice was even, almost casual beside her. She felt no sense of danger in his words.

'What's exciting?' She was smiling, her eyes on the traffic, a warm awareness of him at her side. 'This crazy caper we're involved in?'

'That too,' he agreed easily. She wondered if he minded her driving. Wayne would have minded. She could not remember Wayne ever letting her drive when she was in the car. He had always reached for her keys, if it was her car, and he had been the one at the wheel.

'And what else?' she asked, unaware of his trap.

'You.'

'Me?'

'The way you react to me.' She swallowed and tried to tune him out, to forget him in the traffic. It did not work, his voice was still there, incredibly husky, the words impossible. 'I find it exciting watching you, seeing how I can make you feel so panicked and knowing what's behind it.' He laughed, then there was no laughter. 'I know how you feel, Misty. Believe me, I'm feeling it too. Tell me, how long is it since a man made you feel like that . . . scared and excited all at once because it's so sudden . . . and so powerful? Isn't that how you feel?'

She shook her head, but he must have known that it was a lie.

CHAPTER FIVE

'MISTY DONOVAN,' he said, introducing her to them. 'Misty's been doing some work for me, and I want her to sit on the Annual General Meeting.' He frowned, his hazel eyes turning very dark, and added, 'You'll all understand why later.'

They stared at her, five people scrutinising an outsider. She wanted to run, hard and fast. Except for the secretary, they were all fiercely intimidating people. Helen, the sister-in-law with the perfectly dressed hair, which was sprayed solid and immaculate, her eyes neurotic and cold. Neil, tall and handsome and darkly tanned, the picture of a rich yachtsman poured into a suit for a formal occasion. The mother, her grey hair blued, her eyes soft and clinging, always turning to the men in the family, yet looking at Misty with that familiar resentment. Those three strangers were enough to overwhelm her.

Zeb's hand was at her waist as he introduced her. She twisted back and saw him, and he was one of them: tall and confident and frighteningly well-groomed. She felt his fingers pressing against her back, as if he sensed her urge to run. They could all look through her. They all knew that her suit was a copy made by a talented dressmaker in Mexico for a few *pesos*, that she was nobody and did not belong with them.

She saw Neil's eyes narrowing as he tried to assess her. She saw when he decided that it could not be business between her and Zeb, and seeing his thoughts made her

71

angry. The women would already have come to the same
conclusion. All her life people had judged her on her
appearance, pretty and brainless, and she had never
learned not to resent it, although she tried.

Barry!

He was standing so still, she had not seen him at first.
Either that, or he was invisible when he was in the same
room with Zeb. She saw the accusation in his eyes, and
then her anger helped her remember that this was
business, a game she was playing, a role. Zeb's fingers
pressed into her waist and he was saying something to
his mother. A game. She felt her confidence returning.

She let her eyes pass by Barry, almost as if she did
not know him. He would be wondering, alarmed. What
was he thinking? That Zeb had somehow played his game
and turned the tables on him? Yes, that was it. She was
supposed to have kidnapped the man who hired her. So
she had done that, but somehow Zeb had figured out
the game and roped her into this meeting. Which meant
that Barry thought Zeb had found him out, but did not
know that Misty had. She blinked and wondered if all
life got so complicated for a man who was half of a set
of twins!

'Barry's been playing games again,' said Neil to Zeb.
'He almost had us convinced that he was you.'

Misty managed not to giggle when Zeb frowned with
conservative irritation. 'Let's get on with the meeting,
shall we? This is no time for fun and games.'

Barry spoke then, for the first time, stopping them as
they filed into the boardroom. 'I really don't think that
we should have an outsider in the meeting.'

Zeb ignored his words, his hand guiding Misty into
the room. She had a frightening surge of feeling. She
was losing control, could not seem to go any way but

the way his fingers urged her. She wanted to jerk away, to stop his touching her, sending her left and right, into this room and up these stairs, with the touch of his long-fingered hand. She held herself rigid, frightened by her own emotions.

'What the hell's with you?' Neil demanded, and it took Misty a second to realise he was talking to Barry, not to her. 'Don't be ridiculous! You know damned well there's not going to be anything in this meeting that the world couldn't hear.'

Barry snapped back. 'You shouldn't have worn a suit if it makes you so snarly.'

'Now listen, you——' Neil swung around to face Barry, and for a second Misty could see years of feuding between the brothers. Then the younger shrugged and grinned, and said ruefully, 'Shouldn't we be old enough to drop this?'

Zeb said nothing, and Misty could feel Barry's tension. Zeb's secretary led the way into the boardroom. Zeb guided Misty to the empty chair at his side—as if she couldn't get across the room on her own, she thought with irritation. On his other side, the secretary took notes in shorthand. What was her name? Had Zeb introduced them?

Zeb, as chairman, called the meeting to order. An inconspicuous man named John appeared at the last moment. He was obviously the firm's accountant. Misty let the details flow over her. She was watching Barry without seeming to. He was uncomfortable, and as the meeting went on he seemed to become more and more sulky. Zeb was re-elected chairman of the board, his appointment as president of the company reaffirmed. Neil was vice-president and treasurer. No one seemed to care about that. It seemed Barry wanted no active part in the running of the company, and certainly the women did not.

She saw Barry shift when the discussion moved to the declaration of dividends. It was certainly no surprise to Zeb when Barry spoke up against the capital reserve for expansion in Mexico.

'For heaven's sake, Zeb!' His voice was heated, although she was aware that he kept an uneasy eye on her. 'We're talking about Mexico! Do you know what the national debt of that country is? The *peso* has been devalued again just last month! It's worth nothing! And——'

Zeb said mildly, 'Since we're not investing in *pesos*, that's hardly the point, is it. Are you worried about the security of our investment in Mexico?'

She could see Neil getting tense. He had the look of a hot-tempered young man who did not enjoy holding his tongue, yet he seemed to be making an effort not to get angry.

'You're damned right, I am!' Barry sounded like an excited evangelist. He declared, 'We're pouring good money after bad, and forgoing dividends to do it!' Misty could see that his words affected the two women.

Zeb's brows went up. 'John, could you summarise the capital flow in and out of the Mexican operation for us? In plain English.'

Papers rustled, then a weak voice announced, 'The Mexican operation is directly responsible for twenty-two per cent of the revenue of the total corporation, and eighteen per cent of the costs.'

Misty concealed a smile and Zeb said mildly, 'So, it seems Neil's getting a better run on our money in Mexico than we're managing in San Diego. Neil, about the security of our assets? In plain language?'

What followed involved a technical explanation of the Mexican requirements for foreign business investment and the way the Turner corporation was complying.

'But the *peso*?' complained Barry. Misty decided that the man had the instincts of a rabble-rousing politician. Logic aside, he knew that the two women would have heard about the Mexican debt on the news, and that living so close to the border they would be aware of how the value of the *peso* had tumbled in recent years.

'It doesn't hurt us,' said Neil impatiently. 'Of course we have to carry on business in *pesos*, but we keep our capital in US dollars accounts and our charges are indexed to similar US dollar charges in resort marinas. So the *peso* doesn't affect us.'

'Neil,' complained his mother, 'what does that nonsense *mean*?'

'It means we've got our rates worked out in US dollars, and they are translated into *pesos* at the time we charge them. We take the *pesos* to the bank and deposit them in a day-to-day account, then buy dollars at once. That way, we don't end up holding *pesos* in case of a devaluation. Actually, it isn't that much of an issue. Most of our customers are gringo yachties, and they usually pay in dollars in the first place.'

Mrs Turner snapped, 'I do not like to hear Americans referred to as gringos. You know that.' For the first time during the meeting, Misty heard Zeb laugh.

Then Misty listened, amazed, while Zeb and Neil both agreed to reduce the amount of the capital reserve for expansion by twenty-five per cent. She decided that she would never make a businesswoman. She could not understand why the two men should give in, when they plainly had the vote won without compromising.

'Any other business?' asked Zeb, when the dividend declaration vote was complete. The two women had voted with Neil and Zeb. Only Barry had voted against it, still insisting that the dividends should be higher. Misty thought she heard Mrs Turner muttering something about hurrying up or she would be late for her hair appointment. The accountant was shuffling papers, and Zeb said, 'I guess that's it for you, John. I have one other item of business, but you needn't stay.'

Barry called after the accountant, 'When will those dividend cheques be issued?'

Zeb said, 'On the due date. January the first. Judy, don't take notes on this.' The door closed behind the accountant and the secretary's pen stilled. Zeb said carefully, 'This concerns all of us, so I think we should spend a couple of minutes on it.' There was a confused shuffle as everyone tried to figure out what he was talking about. 'You've been wondering why Ms Donovan is here. Misty is a private detective whom I've retained to do some investigating for me. She has uncovered a conspiracy that we should all be aware of.'

Barry's hand jerked, and Misty saw a stream of coffee shooting out of his cup, straight into Barry's lap. She herself only managed to stay still because she was already playing a part, and being very quiet and inconspicuous was her role at this table. He hadn't warned her of this! Damn him! She had not agreed to speak out against Barry at this meeting. She'd given him the tape, to deal with as he saw fit, but he had as much as said he was not going to confront Barry openly.

The silence at the table was palpable.

'What—what kind of a conspiracy?' It was Helen who finally asked the question. Misty thought that was odd, because she would have expected Neil to be the first one to ask.

'It has to do with our employees union. I'll let Ms Donovan explain it to you.' He smiled at Misty and she glared back. He could have told her what he'd planned, instead of moving her around like a chess piece!

Everyone was waiting for her to speak. She smoothed her hands on her skirt under the table. What the hell! She was on stage, so she might as well play the part. She drew a deep breath and thought herself into her best court-room manner, then she started talking. She had observed this and learned that, and the probability was that this would be the next move on the part of the man named Malenski. When she was silent, the three brothers had a heated discussion in which Barry wanted to throw out the employee and the union, and Neil wanted to fire Malenski but keep the union. Zeb simply moderated between the two brothers, then raised his brows at Misty when there was quiet.

'What do you think?' he asked, and he seemed to expect her to answer.

She shrugged. 'I'm sure your lawyers would tell you that you can't get rid of the union.' This had been Neil's argument, and she agreed. 'However, there may be grounds to fire the employee.' Barry looked annoyed, but Neil looked pleased at her words until she added, 'But if you fire him, you'll be plagued with labour problems, grievances and demands that have no concrete relationship to this issue. The man has been an active union agitator for years, and firing him won't get him out of your hair. The only effective thing you can do is bargain with him. Suggest discreetly to the shop steward that this new man be brought into the negotiations, so that all can benefit from his experience in union-management relationships.'

'Actually,' volunteered Zeb, 'I don't have to make that suggestion. The shop steward already made it to me.' She was intrigued to see that he was doodling, and wondered what the pictures were like that came out from his pencil.

'Zeb,' complained his mother, 'I——'

'Yes,' he agreed smoothly. 'I wanted to make sure everyone was aware of the union issue, but I agree we're just about done. Neil and I will hash out how we'll deal with it.'

He closed the meeting then, quickly, and Misty had the conviction that he had only brought up the union issue to give a reason for Misty's presence. While Zeb was occupied with talking to his secretary, Misty saw Barry moping angrily at the coffee he had spilled on his trousers. She went over to him.

'Well, Miss Donovan?' He was grinning at her insolently. He was not acting the part of his more restrained brother today. 'What do you think of our boardroom? Not exactly the most exciting place, is it?'

She smiled at him, a very smooth smile. 'I thought it was very interesting.'

'Did you?' He laughed rather nastily. 'Well, Miss Donovan, I hope you have fun with brother Zeb. Do watch out for him, though. In the end, Zebbie always plays it safe.' She did not even blink, and Barry cleared his throat. 'I must thank Zeb for bringing you. I wouldn't have missed meeting you for the world—such a *pretty* blonde.'

She laughed then, and it was only half an act. Somehow she could not actually dislike the man, although she knew he was very selfish. She said softly, very low, 'But, my dear man, we've met before. Don't you remember?'

He was very still. Nothing moved. Not his eyes or his lips or his hands. He was waiting, and she gave it to him, gently. 'You do remember, don't you? Saturday, in my office?'

His eyes had narrowed. This was not a man who was quick to incriminate himself. She could see Zeb coming towards them, and she had an uneasy certainty that he would not want her to be doing this. On the other hand, she thought it was necessary to really put Barry in his place. If Zeb were paying her, she would play it his way, but she knew that she could not take a cent from him, and that freed her, didn't it?

'You know,' she said casually, 'my partner is paranoid about people trying to put something over on us. He's always thinking someone will use us, get us involved in criminal acts without our knowledge.' Zeb was closer, and he would be able to hear. Barry's eyes were locked on her, waiting, and she could see the uneasiness in them. They were positively alight with green sparks.

'So?' Barry said, and she knew that he was losing control. He had not intended to say anything to her until he knew what her weapons were.

'So,' she said softly, 'he made certain we were protected.'

'How do you do that?' The voice was Neil's, curious and interested. She hadn't realised that he was standing beside Zeb, she'd been watching Barry so closely. 'I've always wondered if private detectives get much of that sort of thing, clients trying to use them to do illegal acts.'

Misty said, 'Usually the clients don't mention that the acts are illegal.' Her voice was light, but Barry knew this was no joke. 'My partner got around it by installing video cameras in each of our offices. When the client comes in, we push a button, and he's recorded.' She shrugged, added, 'Usually, of course, there's nothing worth keeping, and we recycle the tapes, use them again.' Barry's breath was frozen. His lungs weren't even moving, he was so still. 'But sometimes we get one worth keeping.'

'Any lately?' asked Neil, innocently curious. He was her perfect straight man. It was hard to believe he did not know.

She said softly, 'Yes, on Saturday I had one that I'll keep for a long time...conspiracy to kidnap.'

Barry's voice was choked as he said, 'You're not making any sense at all, Miss Donovan.'

'Barry?' It was his mother, her arm reaching for Barry's, her voice rather helplessly clinging. 'I'm going to be late for the hairdresser. Will you please give me a ride?'

'Rather him than me,' muttered Neil, as mother and son left the boardroom. 'Last time she roped me into that, I didn't get free for five hours. Would I pick up this? Would I do that? Would I mind just waiting, she wouldn't be more than twenty minutes?'

Misty laughed, but Zeb did not. He was angry at her. He couldn't have stopped her, but he did not like what she had done. She swung to face him, wanting this over. 'That's it, isn't it?' she asked quickly. 'You wanted the report on the union, and I've given that, so I'll leave now, if you don't mind. You and your brother will want to work out your plans. He's only here for a couple of days, isn't he? I'll be on my way.' She threw a smile past the men, at the secretary. 'It was nice to meet you all. Goodbye.'

She got three steps, walking quickly, before Zeb's voice, unhurried, halted her. 'Wait, Misty. You'll come to lunch with us, then I'll get a lift with you to pick up my car.'

She shook her head. 'Don't worry about your car.' The secretary was blinking, intensely curious to know why Misty had anything to do with Zeb's car. She could see Neil's curiosity, too. She wasn't sure what Zeb was thinking. She avoided looking. 'I'll have your car delivered here,' she threw back, not stopping, heading for that door.

His long legs took him across the room. He arrived at the doorway before she did, although she could not have said that he hurried. Misty looked around, trying not to feel trapped, but he was big and very solidly in the doorway. The secretary was gone, she'd disappeared through a small doorway at the other end of the boardroom. There was only Zeb and, behind him, the long, tanned form of Neil who seemed to be enjoying watching.

'You're coming to lunch with me,' Zeb said quietly. His fingers closed gently around her arm. She could feel herself moving, going the way he wanted. But she had been doing that all morning, letting him control where she went and what she did. She looked up into his eyes and their warm gold confidence frightened her, the more so because she wanted to go with him.

'Let go of me!' she hissed. She saw the shock go through him at her voice. She had to get out of here! Get back to her own place, where she had control of herself. 'You've been pushing me around ever since we got to this building,' she told him, her voice low and angry. Somehow she knew that it was not really true, but she could not seem to stop herself shouting, 'You've touched me and guided me and placed me, and I'm sure it's all been very convenient for you, but I'm not playing. You have *not* hired me. You put me into that meeting, telling me one thing, but playing your own game, dumping that union business on me without warning. You——'

'Misty, don't——'

'Let go of me!' He was a lot bigger than her, but his hand dropped away and she could breathe again. 'Stop trying to manipulate me,' she said raggedly, then she turned and got herself through the narrow space between Zeb and the doorjamb. Then she was gone, and Zeb was left alone with Neil.

'Touchy woman,' said his brother.

Zeb shook his head, wondering what had set her off, why her eyes had suddenly held that frightened look, why it mattered so much to him.

'Are you sure you know what you're doing?' his younger brother asked with a rather irritating note of amusement in his voice. 'You know, Helen and Mother are convinced she's your new lady. Mother's shocked, because you've been having a cool affair with Alice so long that we had all begun to believe that you'd never change. Helen's a bit excited by it all, but also curious. By now she's probably calling Alice, asking her out to lunch to find out if she knows about a pretty, blonde lady detective.'

'That's ridiculous!' Zeb crossed back to the long table, picked up his papers and shuffled them into a neat pile. He was not ready to talk about Misty to his family, not until he knew himself where she fitted in his life. 'You're imagining things. Mother hasn't seen Misty before today. I've only known her two days, and I don't know a damned thing about her. And why the hell would anyone think——?'

'You couldn't keep your eyes off her,' said Neil, laughing. 'Or your hands. You were touching her when you came in, and she never got near you without your hand reaching out. Very casual, not at all noticeable if we didn't all know how restrained you normally are. But she was right, you know. She said you were guiding her here and touching her to lead her there. She thought it was manipulating—personally, I thought you just couldn't keep your hands off her. The lady has knocked you over, and you're in hot pursuit. Just a wild impulse?' asked his brother, grinning. 'I thought I was the impulsive one in this family. This is not at all like you, you know, Zeb.'

'I know,' he growled as his papers went into the briefcase.

Jo-Anne followed her into her office, a sheaf of message forms in her hands. 'Tucker,' she said briskly, passing one piece of paper to Misty. 'He's after the report on the investigation Kenny did last month. He called twice this morning.'

'I'm sure it went out.' Jo-Anne nodded, and Misty said, 'Dig through Kenny's files and find it. Send him over a copy by courier. What else?'

'The Davis thing again. He called, wants to see you. I made an appointment for him for three this afternoon. OK? The library called. The research is complete. You can pick it up. The couriers couldn't deliver the La Jolla parcel. They'll try again tomorrow. Oh, and Mr Turner again. I told him you're booked up this afternoon.'

Misty swung her chair around so that she could look out of the window. 'How did he sound?' Jo-Anne blinked at the odd question, and Misty explained, 'Was he sulky? Angry? Or very cool?'

'*Very* cool,' said Jo-Anne. 'What's up?'

'That's Zeb.' She was not sure whether she was pleased or not. Barry at least she knew she could handle. 'He's the cool one. Barry's the resentful one. They're twins, so you'll have to learn to tell the difference.' Cool? Zeb's fingers against her face, his eyes that glowing golden warmth. Zeb's lips brushing hers.

'I will?' asked Jo-Anne, her glasses coming off so that she could watch Misty's expression. 'Why? Will we be seeing a lot of them? And why don't I just ask *which* Mr Turner I'm talking to?'

'Because Barry might lie about it.' Misty grinned. 'It's like one of those riddles, where one person always lies and another always tells the truth. If the man says he's Zeb, he might be either of them. If he says Barry, then he's Barry.' He was calling her, actually wanted to see her after she had screamed at him like that. She tried not to feel a warm excitement, but failed utterly. 'On the telephone, there's no way you can—yes, there is, actually. Ask him what my dog's name is.'

'And who knows the right answer to that?'

'Zeb,' said Misty, then she flushed at the look in Jo-Anne's eyes.

'I'll work on identifying Turners,' said Jo-Anne smoothly. 'Meanwhile, are you in if they call, or do I put them off?'

'I——' Which? Did she want her life turned upside-down? She was relieved when the telephone rang and prevented her answering. Jo-Anne answered it.

'Yes, operator, I accept the charges,' she said, and Misty stilled until Jo-Anne said, 'Kenny, from Mexico,' and handed the receiver to Misty.

She grabbed it. 'Where are you?' she asked, biting the words back too late.

'This is the international operator,' said a voice, heavily accented. 'Here's your party.' There was a click and a hum, then nothing.

'Oh, damn!' Misty waited, but she knew from experience that it was futile. 'Did the operator give a number?' she asked Jo-Anne desperately. The secretary shook her head.

Finally, Misty had to give up and hang the telephone up. 'Mexico's a big country,' she muttered, and Jo-Anne agreed, then they both tried to get to work. The afternoon dragged on and there were no more collect calls from Mexico. Misty went out twice, once to the library and once to deliver a summons. The second time, Jo-Anne reported a telephone call that had seemed to be a dead line. It might have been another attempted Mexican call, or it might not.

'And Mr Turner called. He says Max is a very nice dog and he wants you to call him back.' Misty shook her head. She was not going to call Zeb, not with Kenny hovering somewhere on the other end of a telephone line. Kenny would not call if something weren't wrong. She hoped it was only money he needed. Jo-Anne added, 'He sent a message to Max.'

'To Max?' She blinked. 'What?'

Jo-Anne grinned. 'He says he's got a T-bone steak for Max, and wants to know if Max will give him permission to take you out to dinner.'

She had to laugh at that, but still she said, 'If he calls again, tell him I'm not back yet.'

She went into her office and closed the door. She was not calling the man, not going to let herself be wined and dined by a man who already had a high-class girlfriend, who had a family who would never accept Misty Donovan. She slammed the open drawer of her desk closed. 'You're crazy, Misty,' she muttered to herself. 'The man asks you to dinner, and you act like he wants you to meet his family on approval.' She had already met most of his family, and was sure they did not approve. Why was he asking her out? She had checked the man out, and he had only the one relationship. Alice Vandaniken. So why was he pursuing—yes, *pursuing* Misty Donovan?

The telephone on her desk rang. She picked it up. 'Yes, Jo-Anne?'

'Not Jo-Anne,' said a warm man's voice. 'Guess again.'

'Zeb.'

'You're very good at that.' His voice dropped and she heard him say, 'Perhaps that's what I like so much about you, Misty Dawn. You're the one person in the world who knows for sure who I am.'

She swallowed. Why had Jo-Anne put him straight through without checking? His voice said huskily, 'I'm sorry, Misty. I really didn't mean to make you feel that I was pushing you around.' She sighed. Damn the man! She knew that accusation of hers had been almost totally unfounded. He put her off balance and that was what frightened her. 'Are you going to forgive me?' he asked, and she was not sure if he was laughing at her, although if so the laughter was gentle.

'I'm not angry at you.' She licked her lips, discovered that she was smiling. 'How do you do it anyway, Zeb? Jo-Anne and Max—they're both supposed to protect me, keep other people away. You got around Max last night, and now Jo-Anne doesn't hear me if I tell her to tell you I'm not here.'

'She's just looking after your welfare. I told her that you hadn't been eating properly, and I was going to make sure you had a nice, relaxing evening. I've got a steak for Max out of my freezer, to keep him happy. How about it, Misty? Dinner…and a little dancing. Soft lights, a quiet evening.'

Was she really going to let him get around her like this? Damn it, but she did want to see him again. 'All— no, Zeb, I can't! I—there's an important telephone call that I've got to—I can't be away from the phone tonight.'

'Honey, you can't avoid me forever.' His voice was uncharacteristically impatient. She heard him take a breath, and then he was calm again. 'I'm not going to hurt you, Misty, I can promise you that. You don't need to run away.'

How did he know that was her urge, to run and escape her own crazy attraction to this man? 'If I don't run, I'll get hurt,' she said quietly. Why on earth had she admitted that? It was only a few words, but they said so much. 'You must think I'm crazy,' she whispered, staring at the way her fingers were sketching Zeb, his smile, that intent look in his eyes.

'Unusual,' he said softly. 'Fascinating. Not crazy.'

'What is it you want from me?' Her voice was almost a wail. How could a voice on the telephone make her feel so shattered?

'Dinner, for now.' He sounded too damned patient. She knew she was being irrational, difficult, and did not understand why he was putting up with it. 'Dinner, and talk. Let's get to know each other better.'

What about Alice? If she asked, it would be admitting something, giving status to her feelings, as if she and Zeb actually had a relationship.

'I don't know. I—Zeb, it's true that I have to keep by my phone. I—Kenny called today and he got cut off. He——' Why was she telling him this? 'I'm switching the office phone over to my home when I go, and I've got to stay near in case he calls. So—I—could you make it another night?'

'Kenny,' he said, the name sounding strange on his voice. 'I looked you up, Misty Dawn. Donovan and Donovan, and the other one is K.V. I didn't see any wedding ring on your hand, so I'm assuming he's not your husband, that you don't have a husband. I hope to hell I'm right. What is he, Misty?'

'My uncle.' A procession of Kennys seemed to move across her office. The old Uncle Kenny, laughing. Kenny, taciturn. Kenny, disappearing and returning as if the time between did not exist. 'He's my uncle, but he's—he's kind of been my father too for a long time.'

'Fair enough.' Zeb did not manage to keep the relief out of his voice. 'I'm not averse to sharing you with an uncle for the evening. Misty, are you telling me that you really *want* to be alone this evening? We can make it another evening if you want, but I could bring some more of those steaks and we could have dinner at your place, within hearing of your telephone.'

Tonight would be agony, watching the telephone, wondering what had happened that had made Kenny call. He did not call in the middle of these trips, not unless something went terribly wrong. She thought of the other call, the man in Acapulco who said the car papers were not in order, and she could think of any number of ways that Kenny could be in serious trouble in Mexico.

Yet there was not a damned thing she could do about it, because Kenny would never forgive her if she went down there looking for him, if she used her skills to find out what he was doing and what had happened to him.

'Misty?' His voice was quiet, slipping in between her worries. 'Are you all right, honey?'

Was she? 'I don't know. I—yes, of course.' Jo-Anne slipped into the office and handed her a message. Helen Turner, waiting to see her if possible. Now, what on earth did Barry's ex-wife want with a private detective?

'Can I come over tonight?' He was not going to go away. She smiled a little, oddly warmed by his persistence.

'Can I stop you?' she asked softly.

'I don't know.' His answer sounded whimsical, as if he were laughing at his own feelings. 'Do you want to stop me, Misty Dawn?'

Did she? 'I don't know. You've got me at a bad time, I think, Zeb. I'm not very sure what I think about anything.'

'Dinner, then? I'll cook, and you can criticise, and Max can growl at me.' He made it sound very homey, just the three of them; a picture drawn in her mind that had an impossible feeling of contentment and belonging, as if he were someone who would always be there for her.

'No,' she decided, and her voice came firm at last. It was an impossible picture, and she managed to push it away before she rang through for Jo-Anne to let Helen Turner in.

CHAPTER SIX

IT WAS late. Very late. She had left the office at five, unwillingly going out on a case that could not wait. The client was an insurance agency that comprised a large part of their yearly revenues, so she could hardly refuse. Jo-Anne had volunteered to stay at the office in case Kenny phoned again, and Misty had gone out, spending the evening following a man who was supposed to be frantic with the loss of his recently stolen jewellery. By nine she knew that he was up to no good, and by eleven she had the name of the fence he had taken the jewellery to, and she knew the probable location of the jewels. She was also tired, and cold, and frantic with worry about Kenny. There was no point in avoiding it; Kenny did not make collect calls unless he was in trouble.

She stopped off at the office, phoned her contact at the insurance company and got him out of bed to tell him where the 'stolen' jewellery was. She promised to write up her report the next day and send it over, and yes, of course she would be available to testify in court if required.

After that telephone call she sent Jo-Anne home. No one had called, and it was unlikely at this time of night that Kenny would call. Misty drove herself home in a black depression, worried about Kenny and frustratingly unable to do anything about it.

Zeb's car. Sitting in her driveway, waiting for her. Earlier, she had promised to have someone drive it back to him, then totally forgotten. She slipped out of her

Corvette, slamming the door so that it echoed against the walls of her home. She heard Max bark, but for once she did not go directly through the gate to release the impatient dog. Zeb's car was empty. Of course it was empty, but for a heart-stopping moment she was rushing to it, certain that he had come, despite her refusal to spend the evening with him.

She needed him, needed someone to soothe the frantic worry about Kenny, and he was the man who was there when people needed him. He would be at the wheel, leaning back with his eyes closed. When she said his name he would turn and look at her, smiling, as if he would not have minded waiting all night, so long as she came to him in the end.

She was insane, becoming obsessed with a man she barely knew. It was lucky that she had said no. Seven, she would have said, and he would have come. He would have had to take a taxi, because she had not returned his car. Then, when she did not show up he would be justifiably angry. He might forgive her for that, but it would happen again, and again. It was the kind of life she lived. She would not change it, did not want to change it, but he would never understand.

Max greeted her with the frantic panting that made her feel guilty. Did he wait for her while she was gone, wondering if she would return? 'Easy, boy,' she told him softly, rubbing his chest and letting him put marks all over her pale suede jacket. 'I'm here.'

She fed him a big bone from the refrigerator. When he was finished with it he came to her and pushed his head into her thigh. She stopped her pacing then and scratched the place behind his pointed ears. The car in the driveway haunted her. She kept going to the gate to stare out and frown at it. They were both on her mind, the car that she should have returned to Zeb…and Kenny who had not called back.

Kenny would not call now. She could go out, take the car back. She would say, Hello, and here's your car. If she didn't do that, she would spend the night alone. She would stare at the telephone and it would not ring, and she would imagine all the things that could be wrong. She knew from the past that she would probably never know where Kenny was, what he had got into. He might call, might request money wired to him at some bank, in some town. She would never know why, and it would never be mentioned between them again.

All the nights of waiting, wondering where he was, never knowing. They seemed to press in on her tonight, and Max felt it too, whimpering and prowling, barking at shadows behind the sofa. She found herself at the telephone, her fingers dialling the number he had written into her book. It rang three times. No answer.

She hung the receiver up quickly. How could she explain calling now, in the middle of the night? In daylight she could frame some excuse, but she could not possibly say, I just wanted to talk to you. Please talk to me, tell me it's all right.

'I'm sorry, Max. I just can't stay still tonight.' It wasn't fair to have a dog and keep running out on him. 'I have to go out,' she pleaded. 'Look after the place.' Actually, Max seemed calmer, and he watched her go through the gate without a whimper. She stopped with her hand on Zeb's car door, but Max made not a sound. Lord, she was neurotic, worrying about threatening a dog's sense of security by going out in the middle of the night! It was a good thing Max wasn't a baby; she'd have him spoiled rotten by this time.

She was relieved to find his car door unlocked. It was the kind of car you had to work hard to open when the doors were locked. It was dark and powerful and comfortable, and more expensive than her own wild extravagance—the Corvette. He had not left the keys in the ignition, or in the glove compartment. She sat in the deeply upholstered leather driver's seat and contemplated the dashboard in front of her. More instruments than an aeroplane cockpit, she thought wryly. She thought for a while before she started searching; she had learned long ago that it saved a lot of time.

He would have a key somewhere, because he was not so worried about it being stolen that he would risk being late for a business appointment if he locked his keys inside. So the key would be outside, but somewhere he could reach without crawling on the ground and getting his suit dirty. She decided that it would be under one of the bumpers, and the front was more likely because the back would get muddy in the rainy weather.

She went to the driver's side of the front. He wouldn't want to have to go out into the traffic lane to get the key, too conspicuous. Preferably, he'd leave it where he could get it without leaving the pavement. She crouched down and felt, and there it was—a small metal container held on to the car body with a magnet. She grinned, half pleased at her own deductions, and half planning to give him a hard time about the security of his car.

Wow! It started like a dream, low and muted, a silky roar when she pushed down the accelerator. She would have to be very light on the throttle! She turned on the radio and found it noisy, nothing she liked anywhere on the band. He had tapes in a holder between the bucket seats, and she pushed one into the tape deck, wondering what his taste in music would be. She smiled when the music filled the darkened interior of the car. Nice. Soft and moody and warm. If she'd had the right kind of background, she would be able to name the conductor and the orchestra.

Thirty minutes later she had decided that there was no way to get into the house where Zeb lived, except through that marina car park, past the guard. She had stopped in the street, near the locked gates that protected the driveway leading up to his house. Peering through the gate, she found his house with the windows darkened, yard lights showing it to be a big, old monstrosity surrounded with well-kept lawns. All that, for one man and a boy! It would be like living in a museum. It was a wonder he hadn't laughed at her little mini-villa, her three-room cottage with the whitewashed walls.

She could climb the gate, but she was wearing a skirt. Her legs would get scratched, her stockings ruined. A policeman would turn up, asking questions, and she didn't feel like dreaming up answers. The hedge looked like a possibility, but if she tried to squeeze through she would come up against the wire fence that was concealed in the green. Of course, she could leave his car on the street, but she would like to park it where he would find it in the morning, waiting for him.

That meant that she had to get in through the marina and the guard. Well, she'd got in once before, and tonight it should be a cinch when she was driving the boss's car! She put the sleek monster in gear, drove away from the marina, then circled and came back, straight down the street and up to the gate.

'Mr Turner's car,' she told the young guard, wearing her most beguiling smile. 'I'm bringing it——'

'Good evening, Miss Donovan.' He spoke quickly, very respectfully. Where had he got her name from? It could only be Zeb. 'Mr Turner's in the spa. He said to go on in.'

The boy left her and returned to the guard hut where he had left a thick pocket-book. When she glanced back, his head was bowed over the book. She faced ahead and concentrated on parking Zeb's sleek beast, trying not to feel her heart pounding. She thought about parking it and walking back out through the gates, but the boy would wonder why, and she needed Zeb. Just a few minutes to make her feel warm again.

He was in the swimming pool, his arms pumping in a slow crawl that propelled him hard through the water. She stood at the edge of the swimming pool with the lights behind her and the half-lit pool in front, the man swimming steadily, unaware of her presence.

She looked into the small building where the whirlpool was, and saw a glass there, his drink sitting near the pool's edge, ice half melted in it. She heard a surge of water and turned to see that he had reached the far end of the pool, under the palm tree, and had turned to swim back. His style was good, his breath hardly laboured when he turned his face out of the water with each stroke. His hair was wet and slicked across his forehead, just short enough that it did not come into his eyes. He came closer and closer.

When he reached this end of the pool he would stop and open his eyes. He would wipe the water out of his eyes with the back of a casual hand, and then he would see her. She didn't know if he would be glad to see her at this time of night, invading his privacy. He swam in the middle of the night because he could be alone here, his own domain undisturbed, and she was intruding.

She pushed her hands into the pockets of her jacket. She had not changed. She should have, she supposed, changing into jeans and a casual shirt. He would notice that she was wearing the suit she had worn to his meeting. It was sophisticated-looking, a pale blue skirt and jacket with a lacy blouse under the jacket. It was a fake imitation of the kind of thing Helen or Alice might wear. She had chosen it for that, not because it was her style. After all, she had been playing a part for him that morning, and she prided herself in doing that kind of thing well.

He did not stop swimming, and she could not seem to turn herself and walk away. She was scared, frightened, and did not really understand why, but when he finally stopped after another four lengths she bit her lip hard when he stood up in the shallow end of the pool and combed his wet hair back with his fingers. He rubbed his eyes with long fingers, the water sheeting off his face. Behind him she could see that tall palm tree, its drooping, fern-like branches black against the sky. He didn't say anything. He saw her. He stepped to the side of the pool, one stride in the water, then she saw his hands go down on the deck, his biceps bulge as he propelled himself up, landing on his bare feet on the deck of the pool. She swallowed, wondering how she came to be standing there, fully dressed, watching a man in a brief pair of trunks walking towards her, the water balling up on his skin. Her eyes fixed on one drop of water on his chest as he got closer, and she had to stop her finger reaching out to possess that small, tight ball of water, to stroke it away from his flesh.

'You'll get cold,' she whispered. He didn't seem to have any plans to move. He was just standing there, staring at her.

He smiled lightly. 'The whirlpool, then? It's warm in there.' He reached his hand and took her fingers, and she found herself returning the grasp, her palm curving to fit his. Then she was walking with him, into that little building where the hot pool steamed. There were droplets of water everywhere on his flesh. She was trying not to look, but her eyes disobeyed her and she could not stop a shiver at the way his muscles moved under his skin as he walked. Thighs. Arms. Shoulders. The bulge of a very masculine breast under a light covering of dark hair. What would it feel like to be held against that chest? Her breasts bare and body aching, her body trembling against him, her...

'You're cold too,' he said, feeling her shiver.

'No, I—I didn't bring my suit.' She licked her lips and curled her fingers tight when he let them go. 'I should go. I just brought your car and I——' She twisted to let her eyes follow him and her voice rose into a squeak. 'What are you doing?'

'Giving you some privacy.' He was locking the door. She should be panicking, locked in here with this man, but she could only stare, her tongue trying to moisten dry lips as he moved to the big window and dropped the blinds. They were alone, just the man and the woman, and her heart was pounding in such a way that surely, she could not survive? Had a woman ever had a heart attack, just watching a man while he walked around in bathing-trunks, locking doors and closing blinds?

Maybe she would be the first. 'I can't,' she whispered. 'I can't just take off my clothes with you standing there, watching. I just——' The world was thrown into darkness.

'I'm not watching,' he said gruffly. She heard motion, the sound of his foot sliding into the water. She tried to penetrate the darkness with her frantic eyes, but there was only the barest hint of a shadow. 'Don't be afraid,' he said softly, and there was the sound of the water slipping up over him, accepting his body into the warm wet.

'Why—why would I be afraid?' She hugged herself in the darkness. How could she be cold with that jacket on her arms? Under the jacket her blouse was thin and silky, but the jacket and the skirt were enough to warm anyone from the kind of November night that San Diego produced.

'I don't know why,' his voice told her, the voice coming out of blackness. 'But you are, aren't you? You needn't be, Misty. Not of me. Truly.'

She heard the water swish around his body. If she went and turned on the machine that made the water bubble, feeling her way to the wall through the dark, the roaring water would hide his movements. There was the sound of his glass moving and she even imagined she could hear him drink.

'I'd offer you some,' he said, 'but it's Scotch.'

'No.' She swallowed. 'No, thanks.' She moved, feeling her way along the round hot pool away from him. Her foot encountered a lawn chair, set there for sitting on, or for tossing towels and clothes. Under cover of the darkness she slipped her shoes off, then reached up under her skirt, slipping her stockings off and rolling them up before stuffing them into her shoes.

'Are you coming in?' His voice in the darkness seemed almost sultry. She felt her way with bare feet to the edge, then lowered herself so that she was sitting on the ledge with her bare feet slipping into the warm water.

'Just my feet,' she said, wiggling her toes in the water. It felt lovely, beautifully hot.

'Coward.' He was laughing at her gently, saying, 'You're the modern lady, brave detective, but afraid to go skinny-dipping in the dark.'

'Inconsistent,' she agreed, smiling at him although he could not see. The water felt wonderful and his voice was soothing the terrible tension inside her. She shifted and hitched her skirt a little higher, feeling for the bench under the water with her feet. Her attention was half on finding a place to support her feet, half on her words as she countered, 'But then, you're not consistent either, are you? You live such a well-ordered life, predictable. You're in this pool every night at the same time. I'll bet you always swim the same number of laps. You—yet you leapt into this scheme to fool Barry, trusted me with your family secrets without knowing me more than an hour. Rash, Zeb. Not consistent at all.'

She heard the water move, and for a second she thought he was going to cross the pool to her. When his voice came it was no closer, but it had dropped deeper. 'That's interesting, isn't it? That we should both behave so uncharacteristically with each other?'

She swallowed, asked raggedly, 'Why did you let Barry talk you down on the amount for that expropriation?' Surely he could be safely diverted to talk about that crazy meeting? 'I thought the whole idea was to get the money set aside, not declared as dividends. You could have put a little pressure on, got every penny you'd asked for.'

She saw a shadow as he lifted the glass again. 'Mother and Helen might have gone along, but they wouldn't have been happy about it. Neil and I aren't trying to force the direction of the company. The others should be considered, but the future of the company is important too.'

'So you compromised, although you didn't have to?' She shook her head. She didn't really understand that kind of fighting. She understood winning, and losing, but compromise——

'Yes,' he agreed, 'but it isn't quite that simple either. We knew that any restriction of dividends would be a battle, so we presented that expansion proposal in a way that—we asked for more than we wanted, planning to cut back and accept part of that. Actually, Barry was so restrained with you sitting across the table from him that he didn't put on nearly the fight I expected. We ended up with twenty per cent more than we need.'

'Oh.' Perhaps she would never understand corporate psychology. 'You manipulated them.' There was no other way to see it, not for her.

'That bothers you?' He sounded thoughtful. 'I never looked at it that way, but I don't see how I could get around manipulating them, not as well as looking after the company.'

'And they benefit if the company does?'

'Yes, Misty Dawn. And the employees. And——' He laughed and said, 'Even the government benefits, because we pay our share of taxes.'

'You're saying that you manipulate your family, that it's OK because——' Because he was responsible for the business and for the people who wanted dividends now at the expense of tomorrow's wealth. He looked after their interests, made their decisions for them. 'I would resent it terribly if you manipulated me like that,' she said in a low, angry voice.

'I understand that,' he said gently. 'After this morning I do understand that. You'll have to be patient with me, honey.'

'What?' She did not want to feel like this about him. Why was her heart doing this? The roaring. The pounding. She felt hot and uncomfortable. She drew her legs out of the water and sat on the ledge with her wet legs drawn up in front of her. 'What do you mean? Patient? Why?'

'I'm not used to women who object to being looked after.' The water swished and she thought he was moving, coming closer.

'I——' She swallowed. 'I—it's the idea of you not paying attention to what I want, as if I weren't a person with my own will, my own rights. You—I——'

He was there, the dark form in front of her, fingers finding her face. 'I was brought up that way,' he said gently. 'My mother—you met my mother.'

'Yes,' she agreed raggedly. 'I—it doesn't matter. It isn't anything to me. You—I'm not——'

'Yes, you are.' His fingers found their way down along her neck, massaged gently where the headache had been growing all night. 'You are, and please tell me if I push you or guide you or—whatever—too much. It's a habit that's kind of hard to stop. I want to look after you because, honey, you need it and I—— But I'm not trying to push into your territory, to make you scared or...to try to change you in any way.' He laughed wryly, said, 'Don't let me do anything that would make you like the other women around me. It's you I want. *You.*'

She shook her head. This was too much. She had come for the warmth of his voice, maybe to try to borrow a little of whatever it was he had that made people turn to him, hand problems to him. Her problems were her own, of course, but she had wanted for a while to feel that...that someone else cared.

'You talk as if——' She swallowed and could not say it. His words had been that way, but if she echoed what she thought, he might laugh at her misunderstanding.

'As if I want a relationship with you,' he finished gently. 'Something that will last. Yes, Misty Dawn, I do.'

She shook her head, but his fingers were making magic in the aching tension of her neck. 'We can't,' she pleaded. 'I can't. Zeb, I really can't handle a relationship with...with anyone. You've got Alice, anyway, and that's far better for you. Really it is.'

'Turn around,' he said, his voice neutral. 'Come on, Misty.' His hands guided her, and somehow she was sitting with her back to him and he was massaging the tense shoulders with a firm touch that was just this side of pain. She closed her eyes and her head lost its stability. If he would just keep doing that, perhaps all the tension would soften and the pain would recede.

'You're ignoring what I'm saying,' she said finally, her voice languid, unwilling to disturb his touch. 'I said——'

'Honey, I have to. I can't agree with you, and I don't want to fight with you. Right now you're wound up tighter than a drum. You must have a terrible headache. Your neck's tight, all knots.' His fingers stilled and she heard him sigh. 'Look, you really need to get into this pool. Take your things off and slip in, let the heat and the water relax you a bit.' He felt her tense and said quickly, 'I'll go. I'll leave the door locked for you, I'll leave you my towel too—so you can be totally alone, and no one will come in.'

It would be lovely, the warmth surging around her, relaxing. She could feel how everything was wound up in her, her emotions strung tight. 'What about you? What will you do?'

'I'll be outside, in the pool. I'll be there when you're done. Just come out, and I'll drive you home. You can sleep all the way home if you like.' She didn't think that he would swim again tonight. He would just sit there in the cold and wait for her.

His hands had drawn back, not touching her now. He was only a dark shadow, waiting for her to decide. 'Am I being silly, Zeb? I am, aren't I? I—could you just go back over to the other side?'

She stood up when he moved away. Her skirt was damp from sitting on the edge of the pool. She undid the button, slid the zipper down. She laid it across the chair, her jacket and blouse on top of it, then her slip. She hesitated, standing in the dark in bra and panties. She could hear him moving, then a roaring as the water started. She wasn't sure whether he had turned the water on to give her the noise to hide behind, or to give her the pounding hot water to relax and soothe away the tension.

Her bra and panties would be wet if she kept them on. Then, later, she would have to dress without them. The silky blouse that she was wearing would cling seductively to her freed breasts. She unhooked the bra, but kept the panties on, a crazy modesty that he would never know because he could not see.

The water felt so good! She slipped down and the jets forced hot water against the tension of her shoulders. Farther down, and if she lay in the water just so, the hot, forceful underwater jet of water pounded on her neck. It was heaven, an ecstasy that could only be appreciated by someone with a nagging, growing headache rooted in tension. Time slipped away and the only reality was the heat, the pounding water massage.

The silence came suddenly, the water fading, then moving sluggishly in a memory of its earlier force. She lay very still, not wanting to move and let the muscles lock into knots again.

'Here, just shift a bit.' He was beside her, his fingers finding the knots and softening them so that she did not even want to protest. The wonderful massage went on for a long time. She let herself float in a timeless pleasure, her eyes closed, until he murmured, 'Much better now, isn't it? The heat really loosened you up.'

She nodded, but her head did not seem to move. She thought about opening her eyes, but it seemed too much trouble. She murmured, 'I don't think I'll ever be able to move again.'

'You don't have to,' he promised. 'Just lie there and relax.'

She sighed, rejecting the impossible temptation. 'I have to go home. I have to get a taxi and go home.'

'No, you don't. I can wrap you in that big towel and carry you over to my house and put you into my guest bedroom. You can sleep until dawn.'

'My clothes...'

'Stop making difficulties,' he chided her. 'I'll look after them. When you wake up, you'll just go into the bathroom next door, and everything will be there for you. You can change and comb your hair and put on your lipstick, then you'll be the independent Miss Donovan again, your person intact. We'll have breakfast together before we go to our respective offices and slay our respective dragons.'

He turned her slightly, so that she was leaning against the edge of the hot pool. She registered then that her wet, almost naked body had been leaning back against his chest. It had seemed to natural, so unthreatening.

'You're manipulating me again,' she said uneasily. She felt him move, then he was above her, reaching down, taking her hands and almost lifting her out of the pool. It was dark, but she could feel the air on her flesh and felt abruptly, hotly aware of his near-nakedness very close to her. Then he draped a big towel around her shoulders and he was talking very casually, as if none of it mattered.

'You're exhausted, and I think you need to be put to bed right away, not dragged all the way from San Diego harbour to Mission Bay. You're terribly worried. I know that, and although you're not ready to tell me why, I can at least do something about the exhaustion. You're tired and I'm not, and I have a great monstrous house not two hundred yards away, with lots of bedrooms.'

She could not seem to move. He was taking over and she knew it was not a good idea, but it seemed so much easier to let him do it. She saw the light from the car park when he opened the door, then he was back beside her without turning on the light in the spa, finding her quickly by her silhouette.

'I suppose it is manipulating,' he said calmly, bending down, then swinging her up into his arms. Her head found a place against his chest. Where was he taking her? To his bed? 'No,' he said as if he read her mind. 'You're far too exhausted to be in danger from me tonight. I'm putting you to bed, not *taking* you. If you really mind, scream or hit me over the head or something.' She giggled and he said, 'Otherwise, I'll just go ahead.'

It was insane. 'I'm too big,' she said uneasily, and he snorted. She could feel how easily he carried her. He had his towelling robe on, and her cheek could feel the thrust of his chest muscles through the terry cloth. They were outside now, walking through the door from the big pool, stepping out on to the path, then on to the car park. Then she was lowered into his car and she blinked, staring ahead at the building she could see through the window.

Her eyes closed. He had left her alone. Maybe he was going to drive her home after all. It would be more sensible. She felt a quiet smile inside, a sense of wonder that she was sitting here, almost naked inside a big towel, calmly waiting for a man to come and do whatever he chose with her. She was not sure why she trusted him so much. She could not remember trusting even Wayne that much.

The driver's door opened and he leaned in, and put some things on the back seat. 'Did you have a bag, Misty? I couldn't find one.'

She tried to remember. 'No. Wallet in the pocket of my jacket. I left my bag at home.'

'OK. The wallet's here.'

The guard did not stop him when he drove out of the gate. He must have had some kind of device in the car to make the gate to his own driveway open, because when they stopped she opened her eyes and the wrought-iron gates were swinging open, then the car was moving again, up a slight hill, coming to rest in front of a wide stairway that had two lions mounted on pillars.

She must have dropped off for a minute, because he was lifting her out of the car, turning to start up those wide stairs. Panic-stricken, she jerked in his arms. 'You can't carry me up these stairs.'

'Easily,' he promised.

'No! I—Zeb, this house terrifies me.' There would be some stuffed servant inside, looking at her with *that* look, making her aware of the towel and her hair tumbled everywhere and Zeb's arms. 'Please!' she pleaded, panic growing.

'The house is horrible,' he agreed casually. 'But I promise you, the bed will be comfortable.' He must have already opened the door, perhaps when she had nodded off in the car. Now he pushed his shoulder against the big carved door and it swung open.

The foyer was dimly lit, deserted. There were no lights anywhere, except for some form of night lighting that showed the way up a long, curving staircase. He started up, and somewhere a board creaked on the stairs, but nothing stirred in the house. 'Does anyone live here?' she whispered, and he laughed.

'Don't worry, Misty Dawn. No vicious servants are going to crawl out of the woodwork. This house is frightening enough without expensive servants making us pretend we're some kind of élite race because we have the misfortune to own it.' Colours were changing. He walked through a doorway and pushed the door closed behind himself. Then she was efficiently dried. He slipped her wet underwear off so casually that it didn't seem embarrassing.

He pulled up the covers to her neck, tucked her in as her father must have done, because the memory was in dreams. 'Sleep well,' he said gently. 'There's nothing to worry about, not tonight. Tomorrow I hope you'll be able to tell me what's wrong, what this mystery about Kenny is. Then, if I can, I'll try to help.'

He had his hand on the doorknob before she stopped him.

'Why—Zeb, why are you so bloody understanding?' She could not think of one reason he should care for her like this. When he talked about a relationship, it terrified her and he knew it. She didn't know why he persisted in acting as if she mattered. 'You should go back to Alice and forget about me.'

He did not answer. She heard the door close, and she could feel herself drifting, losing consciousness. She gave in to the comfort of the bed, the caring of the man, and slept.

CHAPTER SEVEN

MISTY woke slowly at first, feeling her legs moving against cool sheets, the light from the sun invading her dreams. The dreams had been pleasant for once, soothing and warm, and she resisted the return to consciousness. Then the strangeness flooded in on her, the different feel to the bed, the sun hitting her from the wrong side. She opened her eyes abruptly, sitting up in the same motion, taking in the room that had been so shadowed last night.

She had actually let herself be draped in a towel by a man she hadn't known more than two days, taken to this mausoleum he called his home, undressed and dried and put to bed—as if she were a child. As if he had a right to care for her. How could she have let herself cling to him, lean on him...trust him?

She scrambled out of the covers, found the bathroom and turned on the shower hard. Shampoo was there and she used it. Everything she needed. Brush. Comb. Even a selection of make-up, and she used that. She didn't know whose it was, but some of the colours were all right for her complexion, and she needed a bright mask that morning.

Her clothes were hanging tidily in the wardrobe. He had folded her bra and slip on the vanity unit, hung her panties to dry in the shower. It was hard to ignore the man when he was so damned thoughtful! She wasn't used to that. Wayne had been smothering, not thoughtful, and Kenny had never spoiled her at all.

She went down the stairs slowly. Last night Zeb had carried her up them, and she felt a tingling awareness that she had been too exhausted to feel then. She could hear something, low conversation, and she could see the front door right there. It would be pretty shabby for her to sneak out of that door when last night he had treated her so... Her mind rejected the word 'lovingly' and substituted 'nicely'.

There was a trembling desire in her heart, making her feel young and eager. She pushed that down, tried to get herself into the right frame of mind as she followed the muted sounds of conversation. Friendly, that was what she wanted to be. Just friendly, because he seemed to have got himself into her life and it would be good to have a friend she could trust.

Trust. That was a frightening concept to Misty. She found the right doorway and felt a sudden terror. She had assumed that Zeb would be there, and somehow he would say casual words that made her presence here seem ordinary and right. But there was only Neil and a boy that had to be Neil's son, Keith. They were both looking at her, staring, and it was obvious that her presence was a complete surprise to them.

Damn! If this were a job, she would know her role and play it without any discomfort, even enjoy the game. But this was *real*, and she was terrified when people looked at her like that. She knew she did not belong, and they knew it too.

Keith was staring at her, a gangly teenager who had grown too fast and was all elbows and angles, the shadow of a new moustache faint above his lip. Neil was dressed more casually than he had been at the meeting, wearing a T-shirt that exposed his heavy muscles. His hair was unruly where yesterday it had been brushed into submission. He did not look like the kind of man one would expect to find in this dark, formal house. Even the table they sat at was intimidating, dark and heavy; it looked as if it had been built by a master craftsman of the last century. And lush carpet on the floor, for heaven's sake! Who cleaned it when someone spilled a drink or dropped the soup?

Neil recovered from his surprise first. 'Good morning, Misty.' He was not the kind of man who used formality, and she found herself smiling when he grinned at her. 'There's toast, and cereal. We're not into heavy breakfasts, although I can cook you an egg.'

'He'll poison you,' warned Keith. There was no masking the curiosity in the boy's eyes. They must both think that she had slept with Zeb last night. Why else would she be here? She swallowed, moved two steps further into the room, and felt her body flushing as if Zeb Turner had been caressing it, bringing her to wild ecstasy in his arms. She tried to tell herself that she was a modern woman, that what they thought did not matter. It was a lie. Under the modern exterior, Misty had always had a deep, painful shyness.

'I'm not hungry.' She wanted to say words that would get her out of here, but Neil had got up and was holding a chair for her. Somehow she found herself sitting in it, her eyes staring across at the boy.

'Coffee,' said Neil, and a cup appeared. She watched him pour steaming coffee from a pot.

'Thanks. That's lovely.' She lifted the cup. She did not belong here, and she would get out as soon as she decently could. Drink the coffee, say a polite goodbye, then get out and over to the marina where surely she could get the guard to call her a taxi.

Neil was introducing his son, and she was making the right noises somehow. 'Is your name really Misty?' asked Keith with sudden curiosity.

'Sort of,' she agreed, and found herself explaining about her name. She didn't know why she explained. She never had, except to Zeb. To other people, she always agreed that yes, it was a strange name, but it was hers. Then she asked Keith about school, and the marina in Mexico where he lived when he was not in San Diego.

Keith opened up slowly at first, then the boy was talking almost non-stop, his face animated as he told her about Mexico, about San Diego, about the woman his father was going to marry and how they had met at a crew party in Victoria, Canada, and how Serena had saved his father in an accident at sea and brought him safely to San Francisco. It sounded like a wild adventure, and Misty was not at all sure of the details after listening to Keith's confused account, except that Neil's eyes were warm, as if it were all true.

'School,' the boy said abruptly. 'Gotta go, or I'll be late!' He pushed his chair up and barely caught it before it went crashing over backwards. ''Bye, Misty. S'long, Dad. S'ya later.'

The room seemed unnaturally quiet with him gone. 'What kind of magic did you use to do that?' asked Neil with a puzzled smile. 'That boy of mine is usually taciturn as hell. I can't remember hearing him talk that much in years.'

'Misty's magic.' It was Zeb's voice, deep and amused, behind her. Then he was beside her, pulling out the chair Keith had just vacated. 'No one can resist this lady's magic. Good morning, Misty Dawn, did you sleep well?' Somehow, without saying anything, Zeb's casual question made it plain that wherever Misty had slept, it had not been in the same bed as Zeb. She saw Neil's eyes acknowledge the information.

'Yes, thanks. Thanks for saving me the long ride home.'

'Any time,' he said, and although his voice seemed casual his eyes were not, and she had to curl both hands around her cup to keep it from spilling. 'Are you flying back to Mexico today?' Zeb asked his brother.

'Yeah, tonight. I was going to take the station wagon, if that's OK, and take Keith to the airport. We'll have dinner together downtown, then Keith can bring the station wagon back.'

Zeb laughed. 'You mean that he can drive while you're not in the car.'

'It's easier on my nerves that way,' Neil admitted. 'When he's at the wheel, I'm tense as hell, and he gets mad because I don't trust his driving.' He frowned wryly at Misty and explained, 'He's a good driver, but I guess I have trouble letting him grow up, and sitting in the passenger seat while he drives is the hardest part.'

Misty found herself teasing Neil. 'I thought you were spending all your time in Canada these days? I'm surprised to find you flying to Mexico.'

He flushed, but didn't seem to mind her teasing. Zeb said, 'Don't let him fool you, Misty. He's going to Mexico to make sure the place didn't fall apart, but next weekend he's flying to Canada. Imagine it, flying almost two thousand miles for two days!'

Neil seemed to be used to the teasing. 'Why not, when I've got such a reward at the other end? Keith's coming with me, flying to Canada for Thanksgiving with Serena. I guess I'll keep the airlines busy till Christmas. Then Serena's joining me. We're getting married in Puerto Escondido at Christmas. You're invited, of course.'

'I'd have thought you'd get married here, in this house.' Serena. What a name! The woman would be like the other Turner women, frighteningly poised and upper class.

Neil was laughing and Zeb explained, 'Serena only agreed to marry Neil when he promised to keep her away from our mother. If the wedding were here, Mother would descend and take it over.'

'Would she ever!' Neil agreed fervently. 'Much as I love my mother, she can be a royal pain. Serena is not exactly a serene girl, and she's given me fair warning that she won't be responsible for her behaviour if she spends much time with my mother. We'll have the wedding in Mexico. Mother will come, stay in a high-class hotel, and leave quickly before she's forced to drink Mexican water or eat Mexican food.'

'I'll have the privilege of getting her safely in and out of the country,' Zeb complained good-naturedly. 'She'll argue with the taxi driver, even though they can't understand her English. She'll want *filet mignon* the way they do it in the States, and complain loudly when she can't have it.'

'And you'll smooth everything over for her,' finished Misty.

Later, as he drove her to her office, he said, 'Do you think it's wrong for me to smooth things over for my mother?'

She shrugged. 'And your sister, and everyone else in your family. And me,' she added honestly, 'last night. Thank you. But they all take advantage of you. You do too much for them. Your mother's a grown-up woman; why can't you let her get out of her own scrapes?'

He shrugged. They had stopped at a junction, Zeb's eyes watching the traffic. She liked the way he drove, relaxed and under control. 'She's my family. Don't you do things for your family?'

No. There was only Kenny, and what would he allow her to do for him? 'What do they do for you?' she asked angrily. 'Your mother? Or Helen?'

He shrugged. 'I'm not going to change them. What do you want me to do, declare war? They're my dependants.'

'Everybody's your dependant!' Why was she so angry? And what was she trying to tell him? Not to be a nice man? She felt suddenly ashamed of herself. 'I'm sorry. I—maybe I'm just feeling a bit of sour grapes. My family——' Lord, was she feeling sorry for herself? That was insane. She had a career she loved, a home she loved, and Max.

And Kenny?

Zeb must have looked up the address for her office, because he was parking in exactly the right place. He turned the engine off and shifted in his seat to face her, his hand brushing the curls at her ear.

'Some time you'll tell me about it,' he said softly. She shook her head and he insisted, 'Yes, you will, Misty. When it's time. Do you need your car during the day?' She shook her head and he said, 'Good. I'll pick you up here, then, and we'll have supper together.' She frowned and he said, 'At your place.'

'I'm a rotten cook.' She stared out of the window, watching an old man walking slowly along the pavement.

'I'm not. I'll do the cooking.'

She took in a slow, deep breath. 'Zeb, how can I——?' Hell, she was scared! 'No. Please, no,' she whispered.

He was very still, his hands on the wheel, eyes staring ahead. She was a little afraid to move, to give in to her impulse and run. After a long moment he sighed and said, 'All right. We'll take it slower, then. When do you take lunch?'

'I don't always.' He looked at her and she bit her lip, unable to suppress a smile. 'Are you going to tell me I shouldn't skip meals?'

'Yes.' She giggled and he said, 'I'll pick you up at ten past twelve.'

Later she was glad that she had not refused. It was those daily lunches that saved her sanity, because the days went on and Kenny did not call. Thursday. Friday. Saturday. Then her week was over and she had Sunday alone. She refused when Zeb invited her out on Sunday, refused to let him come to her home. She spent Sunday alone, miserable. The telephone rang twice and it was not Zeb either time. It wasn't Kenny either.

She almost called Zeb as the long afternoon stretched out, but she was afraid to be alone with him. She was so worried about Kenny, she knew she was dangerously vulnerable. Perhaps even the lunches were dangerous, but she could not give them up. On Monday, when he came to her office just after twelve, she felt her heart warm and the sky outside brighten. And what harm was there in it? They ate and talked and laughed about silly things, and he never asked anything dangerously personal.

He talked about his family a lot, asked her advice about his nephew Julian. It made her feel almost part of the family, talking about the teenage boy and his problems, watching Zeb consider her advice as if it were important to him. He did not ask about her family, as if he knew she did not want to answer.

She came to need that lunch hour each day. Without it she would be climbing the walls, because the week went on and there was still no word from Kenny. More than two weeks now. He had never been that long before! Then it was three weeks. By Thursday lunchtime she could not eat anything. She pushed the food around and Zeb managed to raise a smile but not a laugh.

'What?' she asked, blinking, staring at him across the table.

'I asked if you ever eat anything except at our lunches.' He reached across and took her hand, turning it and probing her wrist. He seldom touched her now. The contact went through her like a shock. 'Misty, you're losing weight. You're worried, and I wish you'd tell me about it.' She stared at the table and he sighed. She wondered why he persisted in bothering with her, but he said, 'I'm coming to your place for supper tonight.'

She stared at him, unable to fight. He smiled, an oddly sombre smile. 'You can't get rid of me, you know, unless you can make me believe you don't enjoy my company. You can't, can you?'

She shook her head unwillingly.

'And wouldn't you like to have supper with me? Down deep, wouldn't you enjoy that?' She must have nodded, because he said, 'I'll pick you up at your office at five o'clock.'

She wasn't sure whether she was frightened or happy. She went back to the office in a slight daze. 'Nothing,' said Jo-Anne before she could ask. 'He hasn't called.'

Then her day got hectic. The police station called, asking her to give a statement about the insurance scam. The jewels had been recovered from their hiding-place, and the man who had thought he was half a million dollars richer was in jail.

'He'll make bail,' the policeman told her, 'but we've got him. He's not going to beat this rap. Just be careful you don't walk down any dark alleys before the trial.'

She grinned at that, because this criminal was not the kind to use violence, and she would be willing to bet she was quicker and fitter than he was. When she was leaving the police station and driving away, she thought about Zeb and the smile disappeared. He had not thought of that aspect of her life. Being a private detective was usually no more dangerous than being a librarian, but there were moments. A man like him would never accept that in a woman, would he?

Just what was she to him? What did he want her to be? There was still Alice Vandaniken. He never mentioned her, but the woman was very real, and Misty could never compete with that kind of class and poise. What if he wanted an affair, and—well, be honest, she might want it too. He made her heart tremble, and she was feeling desires she had never really experienced before, not even with Wayne. What if she clung to Zeb, begged him to stay, never to leave her? He would be embarrassed, and she would die watching the affection in his eyes turn to impatience.

Could she share him with Alice?

No! It was not going to come to that. The lunches were just friendly, two friends. Dinner tonight would be like that, a friendly meal, close and warm. Then he would drive away, and maybe she would go to dinner with him sometimes, but she would keep him away from her house after tonight.

No matter how she tried to dampen her anticipation, she spent the afternoon with the warm knowledge that Zeb would come for her at five. She was in and out, going from paperwork in the office to small jobs outside that took up time. Sometimes she almost forgot Kenny, but the promise of an evening with Zeb was with her every moment. She came back late in the afternoon and took two long telephone calls from clients, then saw a new client in her office.

Then Zeb was there, standing in the doorway to her private office and taking it in. It was a nice office with the view through her window and the big old desk that she loved. There was a big painting of a cactus on the wall, and she was pleased that he seemed drawn to it. He had not been in here before. Jo-Anne had always buzzed when he came to lunch, and she went out to him. She watched him exploring her office. She liked the way he wore a suit, as if he were comfortable in it, as if it could not mask his own strong, warm personality.

'Hi,' she managed, and she could not suppress the smile that must have told him how good he looked to her.

'Hi, honey.' His eyes had found the inconspicuous hole in the wall. 'Are you recording me?'

'No. I wouldn't do that.' His brows went up and she said, 'I don't like recording people. It's sneaky, and although Kenny says we should, I only do it if there's a reason.' She smiled when he chose the comfortable chair. 'Barry picked the other seat,' she told him. There was nothing about the two men that was the same, except for superficial looks.

He made himself comfortable, stretching his legs out, leaning back in the chair. 'Why did you decide to record Barry?'

'I don't know.' She caught herself doodling, and something about the way his face took shape revealed more about her feelings than she was comfortable with.

She dropped the pencil. 'Something about him. I didn't trust him.'

'I know the feeling,' he said wryly. 'What about me, Misty? Do you trust me?'

She had trusted him to carry her from the whirlpool to his house, but he was asking more than that. She said uncomfortably, 'It's dangerous, trusting people.'

'Yes,' he agreed, as if it didn't matter. He stood up, said, 'Are you ready? Shall we go?'

He followed her car. They stopped at a supermarket along the way, walked through the aisles together and picked out their dinner. Zeb selected two big steaks. 'I can't eat all that!' she protested, laughing.

He covered her hand where it held the cart. 'Max can have what you don't eat. You can't forget Max!' She picked out some mushrooms and tomatoes, and he added a lettuce and an onion. She grabbed a small container of ice-cream, and he said triumphantly, 'I knew you'd give in to that sweet tooth before we got out of here!'

It was fun, an ordinary kind of sharing that had a crazy, wonderful joy to it. They drove the groceries to her home, and when she opened the gate Max jumped up on both of them, as if Zeb belonged to her home. Then he started organising dinner in her kitchen as if he did it every day, pushing Max away gently when he smelled the steaks.

'Patience, Max. It'll come.' He had taken off his jacket and rolled up his sleeves so that she could see the way the light hairs on his arms curled around the muscles. He was very well-built for a man who spent most of his time in an office. She supposed he kept himself in shape with the swimming. She wanted to touch him, to feel those strong arms closing around her, loving her.

She was standing, watching him, saying uncomfortably, 'I should help you. Is there something I can do?'

'Go and change into something comfortable.' He peeled the onion and deftly halved it with a big butcher's knife, then started chopping it into small pieces. 'Then take this mutt out on the beach and try to get him to forget there's red meat in here.'

She changed into jeans and an oversized blouse, then grabbed Max and forcibly dragged him outside. Once outside, Max co-operated and they walked along the beach, Misty leaving her sandals at the steps to her patio and walking barefoot in the sand. She felt happy, excited about going back and finding Zeb still there, a lovely steak dinner prepared for her.

'No one's ever done this for me before,' she said when he seated her at her own table. 'It's lovely.' He had moved the table out to the patio, and they were eating facing the sunset over the ocean.

'I'll have to do it more often, then.' It sounded like a promise. She frowned, and he carved the bone out of his steak and tossed it towards Max. The dog scrambled madly for it, then carried it on to the beach where he could be heard growling and attacking the bone with ferocious enjoyment.

'That's not very classy,' she told him, laughing. 'Wouldn't your mother be shocked at your feeding the dog from the table?'

'Definitely,' he agreed. 'Luckily, my father was quite a reasonable human being, so I'm not too overwhelmed by my mother's crazy standards.'

'Your house is,' she said, knowing it was the kind of thing she should not say. 'I'm terrified of your house. It's old and rich and very uncomfortable.'

'Yours is better.' He grinned at her around a mouthful of steak. 'You wouldn't consider sharing it with me, would you?'

'I——' He was joking, of course. She dropped her eyes away from him, tried to cut a piece from her steak without trembling too badly. Dinner with him every night. Reading a book, looking up and seeing him reading his book on the other side of the room. Waking up with Zeb at her side, in her bed. 'It's too small,' she said desperately.

'That's not irredeemable,' he said easily, and she really had no idea what he meant. He shrugged, and she knew that he was joking when he let it go and said casually, 'I saw Julian again last night. I think we're weaning him away from the crowd.' He said 'we' as if she had been there, too, not just sitting on the sidelines giving advice. Then he said, 'Julian said something about his mother coming to see you, to talk to you?'

She played with the piece of steak she had cut. If she put it into her mouth, it might choke her. She wished she had said nothing at all to Helen. 'She—she came a couple of weeks ago. Just after the meeting. She wanted me to talk to you for her, to ask you to do something for her.'

He frowned, his hands stilling over his plate. 'Why? Why would she come to you? Why not come to me herself?' And why had she not talked to him? He had not asked that yet, but he would.

'I don't know. I—she seemed to think I would have some influence. I told her—I explained to her that she had the wrong idea. I—well, I told her I couldn't do anything for her.'

'You told her to come to me?' He knew there was something more. His frown deepened the lines around his mouth. She realised for the first time that he might have a difficult temper behind all that self-controlled calmness.

'No, not exactly.' Her salad was starting to look like Chinese food, she had moved the pieces around so much. It was inevitable, of course. She wasn't the right kind of person for his kind of world. It had been lovely, but it was not going to last.

'Not exactly?' He put his knife and fork down, leaned on the table, staring at her as if he could see into her mind. 'What *exactly* did you say? And what did she want?'

She pushed the plate away. She might as well get it over with. 'She wanted more money. She said Barry wasn't giving her enough alimony, that she needed more because Julian needed it. He needed a bigger allowance and it was Barry's responsibility. I—I asked her why she didn't talk to Barry if it was his responsibility, and she said you'd always looked after talking to Barry for her, that it was impossible for her to talk to him. Only this time she was nervous of asking you, because she'd just asked you for money and you'd loaned it to her and...'

'And?' His voice was carefully neutral, and she had a premonition that he was holding back anger, waiting to find out if it was justified. 'Helen didn't call me. What did you tell her?'

She could feel the next few minutes as if they had already happened. He would stand up and walk out, and she would be alone, trying to explain to Max why the man had gone and left them alone.

'Misty?' He sounded like a judge. She shivered.

'I told her—I said that it was time she woke up and looked around. That if Julian needed more money she should look at why, that he needed her attention because he was at a dangerous age, that money wouldn't solve the problems he was getting into. Then I told her to—I told her that if she needed more money from Barry she should ask Barry, but that she was being a wimp, a parasite, living off the Turners simply because she could get away with it, because you were letting her. Why didn't she go out and get a job and look after herself? She——'

'Who the hell gave you the right to talk to her like that?' She watched him push the chair back, winced as she saw it falling. 'She's been hurt,' he said angrily. 'Helen's a victim of Barry's selfishness, and she's entitled to whatever she needs from the Turners. What business had you making her feel guilty about that? She's got all she can handle with that boy of hers. You know that. He's in trouble and she half knows it, and she's worried sick. She——'

'Then she should damned well *do* something!' She shook her hair back and felt the anger and the fear surging through her, loosening her tongue so that she heard herself shouting at him with a horrified sense of resignation. 'So she's a victim! We're all victims, damn it! I'm a victim, too, but I'm not crying to you about it. She'll always be a victim if she doesn't get her act together and stop expecting other people to solve all her problems.'

'You wouldn't understand that, would you?' She had never heard his voice raised before, but there was a terrible anger, a painful power to the resentment in his eyes. 'You don't know about letting people help you, do you? You're determined to go it alone, to get from here to your damned grave without ever letting anyone closer than arm's length away. In the middle of a great big world filled with people who need closeness, you're determined to be alone all your life.'

'No,' she whispered.

'Yes!' He pushed his plate back. There was no reason for the angry movement, except that it made a noise and he could not seem to stay still. 'She came to you for help. Why didn't you think of helping her? You know something about what Julian's into! Couldn't you have offered some help for her?'

She winced, but he laughed, a terribly harsh sound. 'You know, I had a crazy idea about you, Misty Donovan. I thought you were warm inside, and loving. I must have been seeing things, but when I looked at you I saw this passionate, caring woman trapped behind those nervous eyes. I even thought of what you do as a way for you to express your warmth. You help people who are in trouble. I thought of it that way. I suppose that was pretty naïve of me.'

She shook her head. That seemed to be all she could do, that motion of her head in a silent denial of his anger. 'Give my steak to Max,' he said. He looked tired suddenly, and his voice had lost all the anger. Now he sounded indifferent, as if he could not be bothered with her any more.

He was turning around and she could feel it tearing inside her. He was walking out and he would never be back. Max came scrambling on to the patio, came to rest beside Zeb, staring up at him with a whimper that sounded like the way Misty felt. Zeb put his hand on the dog's head in a silent caress that somehow emphasised the fact that he would not come to Misty, would not touch her. She felt all the times his fingers had brushed her hair away from her face, remembered the time that he had kissed her. How could it hurt like this? Could she come to love him like this in less than three weeks?

Love?

She watched him go and she could not move. Then she had to grip the edge of the table to keep herself from running after him and begging. She felt the pain when the door slammed, as if he had shut it on her heart. How could it be like this when they had never been intimate, when he had never possessed her body and shared her passion? Max whimpered and she felt her own tears on her face.

'I'm sorry, Max.' She gulped and tried to make her voice light. 'You shouldn't have liked him so much, Max. Neither of us should. He'll go back to Alice and... Oh, hell!'

She stacked the plates, scraped the steaks into Max's bowl. They were good steaks, had smelled wonderful. She remembered their little dispute at the checkout over who would pay, remembered giving way when he had argued that it would be her stove and her dishes, so he should pay for the meal. They had laughed, and it had seemed easy to compromise with this man. She'd had the crazy thought then that they would never fight, that he would smile and her heart would thunder, and somehow there would be a solution they could both accept.

The telephone rang while she was dragging the table back into the house. She stopped dead, then ran, terrified that it would stop before she could answer. She tumbled on the edge of the carpet and reached for the telephone, ending up leaning against the wall with the receiver in her hand, gasping, 'Hello? Zeb?' before she realised there hadn't been time for him to get home yet.

'Señorita Donovan?' Cultured Mexican, she decided at once. Wealthy, or a professional. Then everything flew out of her head except the fear for Kenny.

CHAPTER EIGHT

ZEB'S fingers grasped the receiver, but she fought when he tried to take it from her. He touched her shoulder with his other hand. 'Misty, take it easy.'

Her grip slackened. 'What are you doing here?' He had gone, the door slammed hard and forever.

'I heard the telephone. You were speaking Spanish, so it wasn't your uncle himself, was it?'

She shook her head, then a spasm distorted her face and she scrambled to her feet. 'I've got to go.' She felt wild, torn, unable to know which way to run.

'By car?' he asked. 'My Spanish isn't as quick as yours, but that's what you said on the telephone, isn't it? You could fly and it would be far quicker, only two hours from the airport.'

'No.' She swallowed. 'Kenny says I've got to come by car.'

His hand, restraining her. She jerked away as he demanded, 'Why, for heaven's sake? What does he want of you? What reason could there be not to fly? How can he ask you to hop in your car and drive all the way to La Paz? Did he explain why?'

'If you're going to shout at me, why don't you just go away?' She pushed her hair back. 'Go away! My life isn't for you.' She pushed her hands into her jeans pockets. He didn't move and she had to squeeze to get past him, heading for the door.

'Misty, for pity's sake, stop and think!' He did not touch her. If he had, she thought she would have screamed. 'Do you realise what that Baja highway is like? Do you know how far he's asking you to drive? It's a thousand miles, for heaven's sake! Take a plane. I can fly you.'

She stopped. She had to prepare, instead of just walking out of the door. She had to buy oil because the garages were few and far between, jerry cans for extra petrol so she would not be stranded on the long highway. 'Fly?' she repeated, his words penetrating. 'Do—you mean you have a plane?'

'I can get hold of a Lear jet. Neil has a friend——'

'No!' What was she thinking? How could she involve him in this? 'I'll drive. A car will have a better chance anyway, and it's only nine hundred miles.' He snorted, and she felt suddenly exhausted. He was already disillusioned enough about her. He had not met Kenny yet. She opened the front door. Her car was there. Get jerry cans and oil—— No, it was too late for the stores.

Clothes... a blanket in case she wanted to stop for sleep... food, something to eat as she went, so that she did not have to stop on the road. She found herself in her bedroom, staring at the wardrobe. She had to get moving, get out of this terrible, paralysing panic. Had Kenny been too sick to call himself?

She took a sweater out of a drawer. The jeans were good. She added another pair, some spare underwear. November. Well, Mexico would not be hot. It would be about the same as San Diego. She added two short-sleeved shirts for driving, a light jacket for outside. It did not sound as if she would need anything dressy. She frowned and selected a light trousersuit that would emphasise the dumb blonde image. Zeb was beside her, still talking.

'...do you mean, *a better chance*? What the hell is that for?' Zeb touched the trousersuit. 'That's not you at all.'

'For the border crossing, coming back.' He did not understand. She sighed and wished she did not have to disillusion him. 'Zeb, if he needs me to bring a car, it's because—he's sick. It was a doctor who called. But he must—he wants me to sneak him out of the country. He can't get on a plane without a valid tourist card. There must be something wrong with his papers.'

She got her bag out and her clothes packed into it, along with the make-up she would need for the charming dumb blonde image.

'You're going to smuggle him back across the border?' He pushed both hands through his hair, turning it into a wildness that was totally out of character for him. 'I don't believe I'm involved in this!'

'You're not,' she said briskly, and it was Wayne all over again. 'Just turn around and walk out. By tomorrow you'll realise how lucky you are that I'm not your responsibility.'

She felt the sick pain of knowing she would have to watch him walk out twice in one night. She bit her lip and tasted the blood. It was too much for one night, both Zeb and Kenny. Why didn't he go, hurry, get it over with? Was he going to make this slow and painful?

His voice was hard. 'You're planning to leave to-night? You're going to drive all night? You'll be dead. You'll never make it.'

'I'll make it.' She had to. He stepped closer. If he touched her, she would either cry or scream. She had no idea which.

He said, 'If he's sick, you can't cram him into a Corvette.'

Had Kenny thought of that? What shape was he really in? She had the bag on her shoulder, was on her way to the kitchen when she stopped and her eyes went to his. 'You're right. I—I'll take Jo-Anne's car.'

He shook his head. 'No. You'll have nothing but paperwork hassles trying to get an import permit for a car you don't own.'

Was he trying to help her? Or to hinder? 'You don't need an import permit for Baja, just for the mainland. Stop making difficulties for me. Please go away. I've got to do this.' She shivered. She had to get into that car, get to Kenny, but somehow she could not walk away from Zeb to do it.

'Why do you have to do this?' His eyes seemed to bore through her, demanding answers.

She swallowed, looking everywhere but at him, her eyes falling on Max. 'What am I going to do about Max?' she wailed. 'I can't just leave him, not for that long, and I have to go! Kenny's never called me for help before. Sometimes for money, but... He just disappears, and I never know where. I never know if he's coming back, or if——' Damn! She was crying. She *mustn't* cry! She rubbed the tears away angrily and gulped the lump down.

Where had he gone? She went to Max and bent down to pet him, because he had started to whimper when she cried. Then Zeb was there, wiping the tears away with a warm, wet face cloth. 'Would Jo-Anne take Max?' he asked.

'Yes. Yes! He knows her, and she has a big garden. He'll be worried, and——' She broke off, thinking of a better solution. 'Zeb, you couldn't take him, could you? He really likes you, and——'

'Right now, you need me more than the dog does.' His hands grasped her shoulders and she discovered that his touch eased the pain. He turned her, and said as if to a child, 'Now, go and put some shoes on. I'll arrange everything else.'

She hadn't realised she was still barefoot. She found her shoes, came back and found Zeb on the telephone. 'All right,' he said. 'I'll be there in half an hour to pick it up.'

'Pick what up?' She watched him hang up the receiver.

'Food. Something to eat along the way. We'll take my car.'

'We?' She realised uneasily that he had lost the astounded look. He looked as if he was in a business deal, arranging a new project for his shipyard or the marina. 'What do you mean, we? I told you, Kenny's sick. He— I didn't tell you everything, and you really don't want to know it all. Just go and I'll——'

'What about your passport?' He did not seem to hear her objections. He said, 'Or birth certificate. You'll need one or the other for the border.'

She went back to her bedroom and found her passport. He was waiting when she came back, and she felt a sharp happiness flooding over her worry. Then she was in his car, and Max was in the back seat, spreading sand all over Zeb's perfect upholstery. She should have fought him, but...

'Why?' she asked finally. 'Why are you doing this? Why did you come back? I told Helen off, and you...' She swallowed, stared through the windscreen at the freeway and admitted, 'I'd probably do it again, even if you didn't like it, because I—and you don't really understand about Uncle Kenny.'

'Then explain to me,' he said simply.

She sighed, tried to imagine a conventional man like this accepting Kenny's wildness. 'The doctor said he was sick, and I expect it's really that he was on a bender and maybe got into a fight. He doesn't do it all that often, but every six months or so he disappears, and usually by the time he comes back he's sold his car and anything else he could get anyone to buy. Maybe he's lost his tourist card, or maybe he's in trouble down there. I know he sold his car in Acapulco a couple of weeks ago. The guy who bought it phoned the office and complained about the papers.'

'So you've been waiting for the other shoe to fall ever since that phone call?' She knew what he would be thinking. She remembered when Wayne had met Kenny, and she remembered afterwards. It would be no different now. She said raggedly, 'I don't understand why you're doing this.'

'Does it matter right now?' The car came to a stop. It was a restaurant, an expensive one that she would not have gone to herself, could not have afforded. He got out and left her, then a moment later he was back, putting a big basket on to the back seat. 'Food,' he explained when he got back into the car. 'And a thermos of coffee. And some cider. Max, keep your nose out of that basket! Honey, can I talk you into drinking some of the cider? It might make you sleepy, and you could use some sleep.' She shook her head, and he said, 'Why don't you drink? Because your uncle drinks too much?'

'I don't know.' She hugged herself, and he reached to turn on the heater. 'I'm not really cold,' she said then, 'but it does matter why you're doing this.' She realised as she said the words that she needed him to come with her, to keep her from going insane with worry on that long drive down to Baja. Why had Kenny not called himself? Was he sicker than the doctor had implied? Or had her Spanish not been good enough to understand the nuances?

Zeb asked her for Jo-Anne's address and she gave it, then he was concentrating on the traffic and she let herself watch him. He seemed so strong, so *solid*. There hadn't been many solid things in her life. His lips were full and firm, his face lined as much with quiet laughter as with frowns. Everything about this man was strong, and—and loving. He cared about his family, loved them and was strong for them. He must care for her too, at least a little, because he was talking about driving her a thousand miles to rescue her crazy uncle. If only she could let him look after everything, hand the burden to him and not have to be efficient. She was terribly afraid that she would make a mess of this, somehow blow it for Kenny because, although she was a cool detective, she was not cool now on this mission.

She focused on his firm lips as he asked, 'Have you decided?'

'Decided what?' He had a very nice face. Funny how it looked so much nicer on him than on Barry. She would not have let Barry take even partial control of this trip in a million years, yet she was sitting here, letting Zeb organise things.

Max pushed his nose between the bucket seats, and Misty scratched behind his ear to soothe him as she asked again, 'What? Have I decided what?'

He pulled the car up outside Jo-Anne's house and turned to face her. It was dark here. She could see only the outline of his face, but he was not smiling. 'Have you decided whether you trust me?'

His voice sounded almost casual, yet she could feel the emotion behind it as if she had a pipeline into his heart. The words were hard for her, but she had to say them. She took the dog's head in both her hands, buried her face in Max's short fur, then whispered, 'Zeb, there aren't very many people I trust, and—and there's no one that I trust with—I mean, there are a few people I trust not to lie to me, or not to deliberately shaft me, but—you're the only person I feel I could trust with anything.' She let the dog go. She was exposed anyway. The words had been like a commitment, a promise made to him. She hugged herself tightly and stared away from him.

'Thank you, Misty Dawn.' His hand covered hers, closed on it. 'That's very precious to me.' She felt as if his strength were surging into her, as if everything would be all right somehow. They would go to Kenny and somehow it would be all right. What on earth had her crazy uncle got himself into?

Zeb let Max out, holding his collar while Misty snapped the lead on, then they walked together up Jo-Anne's path, the lead in Zeb's hand. Misty looked at him handling the dog and had to laugh. 'Zeb, why on earth would you want two more sets of problems—me and Max?'

'Three. There's your uncle as well.'

'Not Kenny,' she insisted, her eyes on his, worried. 'You're not—Kenny's not your problem. And I won't be—I just—I do need help now, right now, but I won't after. I...'

He said firmly, 'If Kenny's your problem, then he's mine too.' Her hand was stretched out to push the doorbell and he caught it, his fingers circling her wrist with an iron grip. He was very still. Max was still, too, staring up at the man who held his lead. 'A while ago you asked me why I came back tonight, and I didn't tell you the real answer.' She saw him swallow and her breath stopped. 'Because you're magic,' he said at last, his voice ragged. 'I'm forty years old, Misty Dawn. I'm probably too old for you, but I'm not even going to let myself worry about that. I've been waiting all my life for someone to touch my life with magic, and I'll wait as long as I have to for you to be ready for me. I'm not fool enough to believe that a woman like you would come to me twice in a lifetime. If you want me out of your life, you're going to have to fight for that. I'm not walking away.'

Her chest was tight. The air seemed to burn as her lungs expanded. Somehow, she swallowed, whispered, 'Zeb, I'm scared. I—I tried this before and…and it didn't work out very well.'

He smiled lightly. His grip gentled on her wrist, his fingers moving so that they clasped hers. 'It will this time,' he promised her. 'Trust me, Misty Dawn.' He had not said the word 'love', and yet she felt as if he had: frightened and excited at the same time. She felt the emotion filling her, swelling and trembling.

It must have been his finger that pushed the bell, or perhaps Jo-Anne had heard someone at the door, because it opened and Jo-Anne was saying, 'Kenny? What's happened?' and then, 'Yes, of course I'll take Max. Be sure to call me as soon as you can, let me know.'

After they had left Jo-Anne's, Zeb stopped at his house for a moment. She did not ask why, just sat in the car, waiting, feeling as if the worry were under control now. Maybe she should not be letting him do this, but it was so much nicer than a lonely drive through the night.

When he got back in the car, he touched her hand briefly and she felt as if he had kissed her. She liked the way he drove, concentrating on the road with that relaxed competence. Wayne had been a tense driver and she had always felt tense herself, riding with him. With Zeb, she let her eyes close and told him about the small property Kenny owned near Ensenada.

'Telephone?' he asked.

'Yes, although I've always wished it didn't. We never go down there together, we each use it sometimes for holidays and there always has to be one of us left to tend the shop. When it's my holiday, more often than not I get a call after two days and have to head home to work.'

They obtained tourist permits at the border, then Tijuana disappeared behind them. The quiet was soothing. Zeb reached across and took her hand in his once, his thumb caressing. Her fingers curled around his. It felt good. What would it feel like if they were somewhere still and quiet, not driving? With the pull that was between them in that moment, she knew that she would move to him and he would make her his, his hands teaching her magic and love.

She loved him. The words filled her throat and she almost spoke them there in the dark car, looking through the window at the black-topped highway streaming out ahead of them. She turned and looked at him then, his other hand controlling the steering with ease, his eyes ahead, but something in the line of his jaw softer than usual, as if touching her made him feel the things she did. She had to make a conscious effort to keep the words inside herself. Magic, he had said. Magic, not love. He was offering so much, but she could not burden him with more. He had asked for trust, not love.

She jerked awake when he pulled off the road and stopped. 'What?' she mumbled. 'Where?' There was only darkness, and Zeb inside the car, leaning over her.

'I'm putting your seat down,' he said softly. 'Go back to sleep.'

Her eyes closed then, and she felt him pushing her back. Then there was a soft blanket flowing over her. 'Where'd you get that?' she mumbled. He did not answer, and she drifted away to sleep again, turning on her side and losing consciousness too quickly to know that she smiled when he kissed her cheek gently.

When she woke again, she was conscious of being alone in the car. She jerked up to a sitting position awkwardly. Zeb was gone. The car lights were off. It was dark all around. Why had he stopped? She was sure that she had not slept more than a couple of hours. Why stop now, so soon?

She started to open the door, to go looking for him, then realised that he might have stopped for a call of nature. It would be embarrassing to scramble out and find him if that were the case. She giggled, thinking of that, and wondered how she could be enjoying his company so much when she was so worried about Kenny. She had not closed the door properly, and the light inside made it impossible for her to see out. She jumped when the door opened suddenly and Zeb leaned in on her side.

'Awake? How are you? Sorry, honey. Did I scare you?' His fingers touched her cheek, then he bent down and brushed a fleeting kiss on her lips. 'Where the devil did you hide the key?'

'What?' She was sitting straight, almost colliding with his head as she scrambled out of the car. She could see Kenny's cottage now, and her voice rose. 'Why are we here? We don't have time to stop! We have to keep driving. Kenny needs——'

'Hush! Misty, listen to me.' His voice commanded her silence and she stopped, her mouth still open, her eyes flashing anger even through the darkness.

'Are you listening?' She nodded, her body tense and ready to resume fighting the moment he finished whatever he had to say. Maybe she was tired. Maybe he needed sleep, too. It didn't matter. She would drive all night if need be. They couldn't stop, must not lose time when Kenny needed her.

Zeb said softly, 'It's going to take a while for you to learn that it's all right to trust me, isn't it, Misty Dawn?' She seemed to deflate with his words and he touched her, his hands holding her, bringing her against his chest as if he thought she could not stand on her own. 'Don't worry, love. It'll come.'

He had asked her to trust him, and she had failed already. She knew she could not change that. If he wanted to stay here, to waste hours, she could not accept his decision. 'I have to get to him,' she said, her voice low and earnest. 'I can't stop and sleep. I can't wait.' Damn! So much time wasted. She got her hands between them, her fingers spread on the broad strength of his chest. 'You brought me in your car. I'm stuck if you won't help me now, if you insist on stopping.' She remembered that meeting, how he had arranged everything without her knowledge ahead of time. 'I told you not to manipulate me! I told you I——'

'Misty, I promise you that you won't be delayed even one minute getting to your uncle. It'll be quicker my way.' His hands loosened on her back, as if telling her that she could pull away from him should she want. He held her shoulders, without force, his palms rubbing along her upper arms.

'I believe you,' she said slowly. She knew it was not enough, after she had screamed at him only a moment ago. 'I don't understand what you mean, but I believe you.' She wanted to say she trusted him, but she had just demonstrated that she did not. 'How? How do we get there quicker?'

'I'll phone Neil, and he'll have the jet take off at sunrise. It'll pick us up at Ensenada and fly us to La Paz. There's nothing wrong with *our* papers, Misty. We can fly into any Mexican airport we want on a licensed airplane. We'll be there by noon.' Her lips parted to protest and he said, 'Let's argue it out inside. Where are your keys?'

'Third tile from the left on the front edge of the patio.' If they flew to La Paz, how would they get back? Zeb was bent over the tile and she explained, 'The tile comes out and the key's underneath.'

He found it quickly, said lightly, 'That's a corny hiding-place. Any amateur sleuth could find it.'

Amazingly, she found herself smiling. 'You didn't find it. I had to tell you.'

He held the door open and she went inside. It was Kenny's cottage, but tonight it felt like theirs, hers and Zeb's. She stood on the tiled foyer and stared at him.

'What's wrong?' He touched her face, drew a soft caress along her jawline.

She bit her lip and wanted to cry. 'Zeb, I'm nothing but a mess. I don't think you want me for a—a friend. I pretend I've got it all together, that I'm a successful lady with a nice life, but inside I'm a nutcase. I really am. I still have nightmares about my parents disappearing, and whenever Kenny goes I freeze up inside until he's back. I—Zeb, I warn you, I could end up——'

Clinging to him, smothering him. 'I—I'm scared of—of—of——'

His fingers stopped her lips. 'I know. It's all right. I promise. And you're no nutcase. If you have night-mares, then there must be questions that aren't answered about your parents, or memories you're afraid to face.' He reached and turned on the light, saw her eyes re-flecting the frantic fear of a nightmare. 'Tell me,' he commanded gently.

'I never knew what happened,' she wailed, as she fin-ished telling him about Kenny coming to take her away, about leaving the home she had shared with her parents.

'How old were you?'

She shrugged. 'Five, I guess. Or six.'

'Didn't you ever ask him what happened?'

'Once. I'd imagine terrible things, dream of them. Other times I thought they were searching for me, that Kenny had kidnapped me from them. I gave up on that idea after a while.'

'Why?' He led her through her cottage as if he knew it, pushed her down on the sofa and came down beside her.

'Shouldn't you call Neil now?' Both her hands were trapped in his. She bit her lip and stared at them, feeling the lonely mysteries of her childhood.

'There's time. It's the middle of the night. Half an hour isn't going to make any difference. Why did you decide Kenny hadn't kidnapped you?' He massaged her hands if they were cold in his.

'If he had, he'd have wanted me with him, wouldn't he? He sent me to boarding-schools. Later I knew, be-cause I saw their wills, but I was in my twenties by then. The time I asked him—I was eight. I was at his place for the summer. He—he didn't answer me. He just left. He was gone a week.'

His hands tensed. 'You mean he just left you alone?' She nodded, silent because she could feel the tears. It was crazy to cry about childhood things when you were grown-up. Zeb said harshly, 'The bastard!' She tensed at the anger in him, then it was gone and he drew her into his arms, his voice gentle. 'Misty Dawn, I'm sorry. I'm so sorry I wasn't there for you.'

The tears came then. She willed them away, but they poured down her face and he was mopping them up as if they were precious. 'My dad used to call me that,' she said on a hiccup. 'Misty Dawn. Kenny did too, but not after he took me away from that house.' She should ask him. All these years and she still did not know the truth, was afraid to ask in case he walked away again. She pulled her hands away. 'I'm all right. I'm sorry I cried on you.'

'I know you're all right.' He smiled, and she found that she could smile, too. 'You've got your life together pretty damned well. You're beautiful—not just looks, darling, but beautiful when you smile and when you frown because you care about something—beautiful inside, where it counts. You're smart, and good at what you do. Of course the past haunts you. It will until you solve it, ask your uncle or go and find out for yourself.' He held her close, as he said, 'No wonder you have trouble trusting. Your parents abandoned you. It must have seemed like that to you as a child. And now your uncle persists in disappearing whenever the whim strikes him.'

'I love my uncle!' She pushed her hair back with both hands, her body stiffening away from him to defend

Kenny. 'Whatever he does, I love him.' She gulped. 'He's mine!'

He sighed. 'Honey, I know. I love my twin brother, too, but I don't pretend he's an angel, and I don't trust him because he's taught me that I can't.'

He left her then and went to the telephone. She watched him as he dialled, wondering why it did not bother her that he saw into her so clearly. She did not trust Kenny. Zeb's words were somehow reassuring. It had never occurred to her to separate the two...love and trust. If you loved someone, and you could trust him, then anything would be possible. *I love you.* She practised the words in her mind. They felt warm and exciting, and gave her a feeling that the future would stretch out full and wonderful.

She shivered, thinking of him standing at that telephone, turning back to smile at her as she nursed their baby. The image filled her with a yearning she had not known she possessed. Stop! she screamed a silent warning to herself. Be careful! Don't reach too far, or you'll be left alone again.

Trust, a voice whispered, the echo of Zeb's voice. Could she?

She listened to Zeb talking with Neil on the telephone, and realised what should have been obvious from the beginning. If they flew *into* La Paz, he intended them to fly out as well.

When he hung up, she was on her feet, pacing, confronting him with a panicked, 'We can't take Kenny out of La Paz airport. We *can't*! Not even on a domestic flight. There'll be officials all over the airport, and all we need is someone to decide to check our papers, Kenny's papers.'

'Misty,' he came across the room to her, urging, 'take it easy. We don't actually know there's anything wrong with Kenny's papers. We——'

'*I* know.' She was standing in the doorway to the kitchen area, hugging herself with her arms crossed under her breasts.

He saw the look on her face, that half-lost look of desperation, and he wanted to go to her, to take her in his arms and protect her. It was so hard for her to trust, to give up control. She was not like the others who leaned on him, who asked him to make the decisions and find the answers, get them out of jams and provide the money. She was strong herself, yet he knew that she had no strength for dealing with this emergency of her uncle's. It threw her back into a dark childhood and she was helpless to escape it alone.

Her face was set and resistant. He reached towards her, but stopped when she stepped back. When had he fallen in love with her? It seemed as if she had always been in his heart, as if he had recognised it that night when he'd first seen her in the whirlpool. 'Misty, if we fly to La Paz in the morning, we'll save hours of driving, and we'll get to your uncle still alert, able to think straight. Then we'll find out what the score is. If it's necessary, we can get a car and drive back here, but let's not cross that bridge until we get to it.'

He saw the convulsive movement of her throat, knew how frightened she was for her uncle. She licked her lips, seemed to need the moisture before she could speak. 'But—Zeb, I know you don't like the idea of sneaking through borders and I—I'm afraid you'll decide we should—should turn Kenny in.' She shuddered, wailed, 'Zeb, in Mexico they put people in gaol pretty easily.

Their legal system is on the Napoleonic code. It's not a matter of innocent until proven guilty.'

His fingers curled in the effort not to reach out to her. She looked so alone, and he wanted to show her that she would never be alone again. 'Honey, I promise you I won't take any chances with his safety, or his freedom.' She was shivering, and he wanted to put his arms around her, to warm her. He could not. Not yet. She must accept this without influence from the stirring of senses that their closeness brought.

Only the truth for his misty love. He felt the pressure of tears behind his eyes, and could not remember when anyone had made him feel like this, as if her pains were his in every sense of the word. 'Honey, you're right. I don't like sneaking around, through borders or in and out of airports. I'd prefer to do this straight, and it might be possible. That's why I thought of Neil. Not just because he can get the plane and fly us, but because he has contacts down here, friends who might help.' He saw her alarm and held up his hand. 'Darling, I promise that I won't take any chances.' He grinned, then said, 'You know me. You said it yourself. Conservative. Play it safe—safe for your uncle. I will, I promise. And if it can't be straightened out, I'll help you do it your way.'

He saw the trembling as she smiled, but her eyes lightened and there was true amusement in them. 'I have trouble with the picture of you as a border runner,' she said on a giggle.

'So do I,' he admitted ruefully, and he wanted to sing when she laughed aloud. Then she reached out her hand, and he took it.

Later, after the telephone call, they shared a quiet meal made from the picnic basket, and she could not seem to stop the impossible images of a future stretching out, a life filled with Zeb.

She knew that it was impossible. Their houses. Their lives. Their families. Opposites. Yet she knew that he wanted her, and she loved him. If there was some part of their lives they could share, she was going to reach for it and try to tell herself it was enough. He was standing at the window, looking out at the shadow that was the driveway, his car. She turned out the light so that they were in semi-darkness, seeing by the light from the kitchen. She touched his arm and it came around her, holding her against him.

He smiled down at her. She could see his strong lips curving. 'I like your house better,' he said softly. 'It has a warmer feeling.'

'Me, too,' she agreed, turning and letting her arms slide up on to his shoulders. She felt the excitement flowing over her nervousness. 'This is more Kenny's place than mine. I don't come here that much since I got my house.' His shoulders felt strong and solid. Her thumbs probed gently in the muscles, finding them tensed. She kneaded to try to ease the tension. He bent his head, and she saw his face still as his eyes found hers in the dark. She trembled, her fingers going slack on his shoulders, her lips parting.

It was so slow. Silent...the world still...waiting. Her tongue slipped out to wet her lips. She felt her heart trembling as he slowly bent his head. His arms around her, hands spread across her back. The slightest pressure, fingers urging her closer. His lips only inches from hers. She felt her mouth move as if to urge his closer. On her back, his fingers moved, traced the muscles along her spine. She felt that flesh trembling, rigid with sensation.

His fingers firmed, urged her closer, traced all the way down to her waist, smoothing her body against his. Their lips fused, her body stretched up against his long, hard, lean length. His hands slipped down to her hips and drew her breathlessly close. She felt her fingers curling in the crisp coolness of his straight brown hair, her arms stretched up to bring herself as close as possible.

His lips teased hers, nibbling at the side of her mouth, then covering hers, and she opened to him wordlessly at his silent command. His tongue exploring, possessing the moist depth of her... Tongues touching, knowing the dark need that grew and flowered between them... Wonderful, exciting, warm dizziness... His arms tight and close, her woman's flesh straining, needing, wanting.

Her eyes dragged open as his lips receded, his touch seeming to cling even as his head drew back. Zeb, face somehow soft and vulnerable over hers as her vision returned slowly, seemed to fade in like the special effect of a skilful camera. His hand was in her hair, his fingers spread through it, making her scalp tingle. She let her head fall back, knowing that he would support it and she could look up at him and fill her wide eyes with the glory of this man she loved.

Her lips parted, but the words did not pass them; instead they filled her until she could not breathe. *I love you*.

His voice was low and husky, breathy, as if he could not control the beat of his heart or the movement of his lungs. 'You'll get a sore neck, honey. I'm so much taller.'

'I like it.' Was that her voice whispering? 'It makes me feel...cherished.'

'You are,' he promised raggedly. His lips possessed hers again, briefly, hard, and she felt a hot wildness singing through her veins. 'But you needn't break your neck,' he said hoarsely as his arms shifted.

Then she was floating up, curled against his chest. He was very still, looking down into her face. She let her knees curl against him, her head rest on his shoulder. She let one arm curl around his neck, feeling the corded muscles that seemed to hold her so easily. Her face rested easily against his shoulder now, and she could let her eyes half close without losing sight of the way his throat moved when he looked at her, as if there were a lump of emotion there that he could not shed. Her other hand was free to reach up, to touch the cool smoothness of his cheek.

'You must have shaved before you came to my place tonight,' she whispered.

'Of course,' he said, and she felt her heart crash into her ribs, as if he had made some declaration of his feelings. She brought both arms around his neck and pulled herself closer, her lips caressing against the soft, cool stretch of flesh under his jawline. She felt the touch of her lips make him quiver, felt his arms tense as they held her, and she knew that she would be his this night.

He turned his head and his lips possessed hers, and her world spun away again, dark and starlit and dizzy-wonderful. When the kiss ended, she whispered, 'The door on the right.'

Somehow he managed to open the door without letting go of her. Her lips sought the cool feel of his throat again, searching for and finding the touch that would make him tremble. Then she felt the softness of the bed at her back, his body leaning over hers, and her eyes opened like a flower unfolding.

He was sitting beside her, leaning over her, his face dark and serious. The moon outside showed his features to her. She watched, mesmerised as he slowly freed the buttons of her blouse. His thumbs grazed gently over the flesh above her breasts as he parted the cotton blouse. She had small, firm breasts that did not need a bra. She often went braless at home, but almost never in public, although tonight somehow she had left the bra off when she had changed. Her mind went back hours, to the time when he had been cooking steaks and she had been changing out of her work clothes, and the omission of the bra took on a significance she had not realised then.

'What are you thinking?' he asked in a low voice, as the cotton fell away to expose her naked breasts.

'I——' She could not tell him. She closed her eyes against something in his face, then opened them and found him staring at her body, his hands very still, fingers still curled in the fabric of her blouse.

She did not realise that he had stopped breathing until he drew in a deep, unsteady lungful of air. Then the cotton in his fingers fell back on to the bed. She saw his eyes as his hands caressed with delicate strokes that moved from the soft flesh at her midriff to the white roundness of the undersides of her breasts. He stopped, stilled, with his palms containing the softness. Then he bent and touched his lips to one pink nipple. She gasped, her heart wild with the pleasure of that brief touch. She could feel her breasts swelling in his hands, and her head moved on the bed, a gentle restlessness that was already growing to the wildness of passion as he bent over her again.

'Beautiful,' he groaned, his lips leaving her breasts, seeking her parted, heated mouth. 'You're beautiful, Misty Dawn.'

Her fingers sought the freedom of his chest, fumbled on the buttons of his shirt. She managed one button, then his tongue plundered the depths of her mouth and she could not think, could only strain upward, her body blindly seeking the intimacy it craved, her arms losing track of their purpose and tangling in his shoulders, his neck, the cool crispness of his hair.

His mouth, exploring the curve of her cheekbone, the tender hollows around her eyes, the tingling sensitivity of her ears... Her lips, seeking his cheek, the incredible soft tenderness of his eyelids, the crease that she found in his forehead. When he drew away, her lips tried to follow, sought his until she was sitting beside him, her fingers finding again the buttons of his shirt.

He stilled his lips, drew back enough to watch her as she concentrated on those buttons. Her fingers were trembling. She could feel the unevenness of her breathing. His hands slipped under the gaping front panels of her blouse at her shoulders, pushed the fabric slowly down, watching with his breath held, then ragged and quick. The fabric pinned her arms at her sides. She let go of his buttons and then the blouse was gone, her arms free again.

I love you. The words were singing inside her, swelling her chest to bursting. Her lips parted and he bent forward to take their sweetness, a slow, sensuous touch that made her eyes heavy and her hands restless on his chest.

'Are you ever going to get my shirt off?' His voice was a trembling chuckle. She licked her lips and concentrated on the buttons.

'It's hard,' she admitted softly. One button. His hands possessed her breasts, thumbs stroking gently across the aroused peaks. Her head fell back and her eyes closed as the passion roared through her veins and she gasped, 'You're making it very difficult.'

'I know.' His voice was silky-strong, his hands and body following her as she fell back on to the bed. Then he was beside her, leaning over her, and somehow the shirt was free, pushed away, and he drew her close against the strong warmth of his hard body.

Later, when she was wild in his arms, he whispered unsteadily, 'Don't worry, Misty Dawn. I'll protect you, darling.'

'I know.' She had known. She stretched herself tightly against him, felt his body hard and aroused, needing her. She whispered, 'I trust you, darling. All the way.'

Then his hands were fumbling, crazily clumsy with the fastener at the waist of her jeans. She felt his heart thundering through the air around them when the zipper slid down and he parted the heavy denim and touched the slight roundness of her abdomen. His belt seemed easier, her hands suddenly sure as they moved to his zipper. His hands at her hips lifted and pulled the harsh denim away, leaving her white and trembling in the moonlight, her body naked except for the flimsy lace of her panties.

His fingers trailed across the lace, a sensuous, maddening caress that fed the need for more. 'I shouldn't—we should wait, settle this thing with your uncle first. One thing at a time.' His fingers trembled and he groaned, 'Do you know what you're doing, Misty Dawn? We're pretty close to the point of no return.'

She felt a smile growing. She touched, just a gentle stroking there, and he gasped and shuddered against her. 'Aren't we past the point of no return?' she asked, stretching out the joy of waiting for his possession of her, feeling the tension building in them and between them.

His mouth possessed one turgid breast and she strained against him, offering more. She felt his tongue stroke, its warm moistness curving to her shape as it stroked slowly across her nipple. His voice was muffled, deepened and slow with passion. 'You could scream,' he said as his hand found the warm softness of her inner thigh. 'Kick and scream and try your judo... and...'

Feather-touch stroking where the heat pounded... She twisted and he moved, and then she could feel the roughness of his leg against hers, his knee finding its way between her legs, a pulse beating heavy and hot through her abdomen, her legs, the centre of her womanhood. His touch, there... and *there*! So... so...

'What if I don't?' she managed, her voice a weak gasp against his mouth as it sought hers again. 'What if I don't fight? Don't scream? What if...?' She met his kiss with hers, this time with her own need and passion opening, meeting his thrust, answering it with her own deep and growing hunger.

Then the moon slipped down and shone brightly through the window, drawing her eyes open to see the naked hunger in his face. She saw his eyes and she was filled with a tender passion. She could trust this man. With anything. With herself.

CHAPTER NINE

MISTY haggled with the taxi driver in Spanish while Zeb and Neil watched. She suspected that the driver enjoyed the exercise, and it settled her nervousness. She was gaining control, acting the part of a tourist who had nothing better to do than enjoy the country and practise Spanish by bargaining with the Mexicans. The skills she used every day at work were returning to her today.

Zeb had woken her with the dawn, already dressed. She had opened her eyes, stared into his and wondered what he would say if she told him she loved him. He had touched her shoulder almost impersonally.

'One thing at a time,' he had said gently. 'Get up and have your coffee, then we'll go rescue your uncle.'

He had left her alone with her questions. Did he regret last night? What about Alice? It had been easy to forget Alice with his arms around her, his lips on hers, but Alice fitted into his world far better than Misty did. Zeb would realise that.

They had flown south along the long Baja California peninsula staring down at the barren desert and the mountains. White surf rolling in on the west coast, quiet expanses of sandy beach on the east. Sunshine everywhere. Neil had laughed at that, telling her that the sailors called this kind of day 'wall-to-wall blue'. Zeb had smiled. She had smiled back and felt the blue growing brighter.

She could do anything, endure anything, if he were at her side.

Near La Paz they had flown into an area of greater vegetation, palm trees and fig trees, large ranches covered with big cacti back in the mountains. She had looked at a map last night in the cottage, and this morning she had recognised the largest city on the Baja peninsula from the way it nestled into the southern end of Bahía de La Paz in lazy tropical beauty.

'Not exactly in the tropics,' Neil had corrected, his sun-browned face and dark glasses proclaiming that he spent his life in this land of eternal summer. 'La Paz is just north of the Tropic of Cancer, so doesn't qualify as tropics technically.'

'Close enough,' Zeb decided, taking her arm and helping her out of the plane. It felt nice, as if she were cherished. 'You are,' he had said last night.

Then the taxi ride to town. The driver dropped Neil at an office building downtown where he was going to look up his government contact while Misty and Zeb went to see the doctor. The doctor's office that the driver stopped in front of was a small, quiet building with an attractive courtyard. 'I already like him,' decided Zeb as they walked up the path.

'He sounded awfully nice on the telephone.' She was trying not to sound nervous. The door swung open when Zeb touched it. The waiting-room inside was bordered with straight-backed chairs, unoccupied except for a Mexican woman who sat stiffly against the far wall with her hands folded in her lap. Misty sat and Zeb followed her lead.

'*Buenos días,*' said Misty formally to the woman.

The Mexican woman replied with rapid Spanish. Zeb saw Misty blink, then she shot back a string of words that made no sense to him. By this time the woman was smiling widely, and Misty was smiling too. One of them told a joke. Zeb wasn't sure which, but they both laughed. The Mexican woman held out her flat hand and waggled it and frowned. Misty returned a similar gesture and they smiled widely at each other again.

The doctor appeared. He was a slight, dark-haired man dressed immaculately in a light short-sleeved shirt and tan trousers. His eyes took in all three people sitting in the waiting-room, but it was the Mexican woman he greeted formally and invited into his office.

'We're next,' said Misty.

'Sign language?' asked Zeb. The doctor had not said a word to them.

She settled back into the seat. She had that alert and alive look he remembered from that first night in the pool. She was having fun, he decided. In a moment she would remember Kenny and frown, and the worry would be in her eyes, but right now she was busy meeting Mexico on its own terms and faring very well. She was wearing the trousersuit she had packed. That morning she had told him that it would not do to meet the doctor in jeans, and he had told her that the suit looked a lot better on her than he had thought it would. There had not been time for much else, but he had seen the nervousness in her eyes when they met his, and had avoided taking her into his arms. Later.

Now she said, 'Didn't you see that gesture he made with his fingers? They use it in Mexico all the time. It means "just a minute", but it's usually more than a minute. It's like *mañana*. In the dictionaries, *mañana* means tomorrow, but actually it means "not today", which is quite a different thing.'

'What about the business with the *señora*? All the laughter and hand waggling?'

She grinned. 'We said hello, then she asked if I was visiting La Paz and did I like it, and I apologised for my Spanish and she waggled her hand when she said she didn't speak much English. She told me the doctor was very good, and he spoke English well for the gringos.'

They had a long wait. Misty leaned back against the seat. In Mexico it was a mistake to try to hurry events, and she felt better able to wait now that she had seen the doctor. She glanced at Zeb uneasily after a few moments, but he was relaxed. He had picked up a magazine from a small table in the corner and was reading it. She knew the level of his Spanish was very rudimentary, so he must be looking at the pictures. She should have realised that he would not be impatient.

The dark lashes of his hazel eyes were almost against his cheek as he read the magazine in his lap. She liked the way his hands held the magazine, positively and without any fuss. He was very still, not even the long, strong fingers on the magazine betraying restlessness. For a man who lived a conventional life, he was coping very well with this unpredictable world of hers. She wondered what he and Kenny would make of each other.

'What are you giggling about?' Zeb's brows were lifted in query, the thick, dark line over his eyes emphasising the sudden gold lights in his hazel eyes. Some day she would figure out what it was that made the hazel turn that warm gold. 'You're chortling like a madwoman.'

'Am I?' She giggled again, found her hand curling around his forearm and let it stay there. 'I was just remembering when Wayne came to meet Kenny. It wasn't funny at the time. It was a disaster. Afterwards, Wayne told me that I wasn't to see Kenny after we were married.'

He covered the hand on his arm with his free hand. It was the first time she had touched him since last night.

'But it's funny now? What happened when Wayne met Kenny?'

Her laughter escaped. 'Kenny had been on this case, trying to bring back a runaway teenage boy. The kid was living on the beaches, and Kenny was hanging out with the beach crowd. He was dressed—well, he had to dress the part. I tried to explain that to Wayne, but he just— Kenny was talking the part, too, complete with foul language and weird significant pauses. Kenny really gets into a role and lives it.'

Zeb grinned, then said, 'Your Wayne was a bit of a stuffed shirt, wasn't he? He was probably having nightmares of this apparition you claimed as an uncle turning up at the wedding and shouting when the priest asked if anyone objected.'

'Oh, no! His mother would have fainted if Kenny had done that.' Why had she thought the memory hurt so much? Wayne had not been close, not with the warm closeness she felt when this man smiled at her, touched her. 'I was young,' she said quietly, her smile fading. 'I wanted someone all my own, and—and I guess I didn't look too closely. He seemed to want me, and I just grabbed, and of course it didn't work.'

'I'm glad you've got that in perspective,' he said quietly. 'Just remember that I'm not Wayne.'

He took her hand and enfolded it in both his. Soon, she knew, there would be a time when they would be alone again. She saw what was in his eyes and felt both excited and frightened. Last night he had touched her, made love to her, but she was still nervous of the mental intimacy that pulled them together.

'Zeb, you've got to realise—Kenny might just have done that.'

'Done what?' He caught the underside of her chin and raised it gently so that he could capture her eyes with his again. 'You mean, get up at the wedding and protest?'

Wedding? Why were they talking about weddings? Did it mean anything? She swallowed. 'If he thought it was a good idea, he would. I don't mean he'd do it as a joke, maliciously, but he's not exactly predictable.'

'I'll be on my guard,' he said seriously. 'But I'm not running just because you've got a nutty uncle.'

The *señora* returned to the waiting-room, grinned at Misty and poured forth a quick sentence of Spanish on her way out. The doctor came behind her.

'You are the woman I called on the telephone?' he asked in Spanish. She nodded and he opened the door to his office wider, nodding permission for them to enter. He closed the door carefully, shutting the three of them into the small plain office. 'It is better we speak in English,' he said quietly.

'How is he?' Misty tensed, trying to see the answer in the doctor's face. 'Where is he?'

'He is at Los Frailes.' The doctor gestured in the direction she thought might be south. 'He is staying in a caravan there, at *la playa*——' He shrugged as his English failed.

'The beach?' she translated, and he nodded.

'There is a problem, you understand. There was an accident, and his leg is hurt. I have put stitches and put it into—I have stabilised it. It will be good, but he must go to his doctor, to his hospital. They must watch that there is no infection. I cannot take him to the hospital here. He will not agree.' He frowned, and she realised that if he knew Kenny's reason for resisting the hospital he would not admit it.

Zeb had been silent until now. His hands were casually slipped into his trouser pockets, now he asked, 'Can he travel? Can he be moved safely?'

'Yes.' The doctor turned to Zeb, and seemed more comfortable now that he was talking with another man. 'You understand, it is not good for the leg to be moved too much. He can travel. There is damage, and there may be——' He shrugged when the English word failed him. 'He must not walk, but there will be no damage if he is moved without walking.'

'Can we drive him back?' If he would not go to a hospital, then he would also be unwilling to go to an airport.

'No! You must not!' He frowned, deeply disturbed. Then he turned to Zeb, and his hands were alive with trying to impress this man with his earnestness. 'The leg will not damage, but to drive there will be much pain. The road *todo*—all up Baja California is too much for the leg. There is jets, and he will go best in a jet. Can you go to Los Frailes?'

Zeb answered, 'We have a taxi for the day. How far is it?'

'No!' The doctor spread his hands. 'You should not take the taxi. The driver will remember a customer for a whole day, and it is best not to talk about the man sick at Frailes. And it is too far, the road is not good. There is a small airport. You should find a plane to take him from the airport at Frailes to here where he can be moved to the jet. Tomorrow you should do it. The jet to Los Angeles goes at *las doce y media*.'

Zeb blinked and Misty translated, 'It goes at twelve-thirty,' but Zeb was already asking the doctor about the length of the runway at Los Frailes, and after a quick telephone call the doctor had the answer.

Misty thanked him with the profuse formal phrases that were native to Spanish, asking, 'Does my uncle owe you anything for your medical services?'

He shook his head and said, 'Go well. Tell the American to come back one day and I will have him to dinner at my home.'

The taxi was gone when they got outside. There was a small Volkswagen car in its place, with Neil at the wheel. They climbed in as Misty told Zeb, 'It's more than just a lost tourist card. It's some kind of mess. He refused to go to the hospital. Maybe the police are even looking for him.'

'At least he's charmed the doctor into harbouring a fugitive, and now abetting his escape.' Zeb shook his head, laughed wryly and said, 'I've stumbled into Wonderland, I think.'

Neil laughed at that and put the car into gear. 'Definitely out of your normal sphere, big brother. Where do we find the gringo fugitive?'

'Los Frailes,' said Misty, wondering why these men should be helping her, why Zeb's eyes should soften when they looked into hers. I love you, she thought, and wondered if she would ever have the courage to tell him. 'Zeb, is the runway long enough for the plane?'

He nodded. 'Sounds like it. Do you know the place, Neil? Can we take the Lear in?'

'No problem, though I'm not sure what we'll use for wheels when we get there. I think we'd be better to look for something there, though, and play down our transactions here in La Paz. There's lots of *federales* around, and my friend says they are looking for a gringo. Tall, blond, in his mid-forties. He speaks fluent Spanish and is believed to be trying to get into Baja from the mainland.'

'Kenny.' She closed her eyes. What had he done to be actively searched for by the federal police? 'He's in a mess, worse than I thought. Why are you help-ing——?' Zeb's hand reached forward and touched her shoulder to silence her words.

'Did your friend know why the gringo is wanted?' Zeb asked.

'Something to do with a car. There was an accident, and the car was in Mexico on an import permit.' The gears on the Volkswagen ground as Neil slowed for a stop sign. 'The gringo's name is on the papers for the car, but a Mexican national claims the car was sold to him. They want to talk to the gringo.' Neil frowned, then said, 'Actually, I wouldn't recommend his making himself available. He's definitely violated a couple of laws, and he'd probably be gaoled until it's sorted out. Better if he can get home to the States, then deal with any repercussions from there. It sounds as if he was the only person hurt in the accident.'

'Back to the airport, then,' suggested Zeb, turning to try to get his long legs comfortable in the back seat of the car. Misty had ended up in front, next to Neil.

'Los Frailes,' Neil said as if in agreement to some words of Zeb's she had not heard. 'Then you and I on a diplomatic mission?' Things were starting to move and she had no control of them. She was realising that the two brothers worked well together, and often seemed able to communicate in a verbal shorthand that was bewildering.

Neil asked suddenly, 'Have you got cash?'

'Some. I cleaned out the safe at the house.'

'Should be enough to get on with, then,' said Neil.

Misty twisted, her eyes flying to Zeb's. 'What does Neil mean, diplomatic mission? I should go too.'

'Definitely not!' said Neil.

Zeb explained, 'You're related to Kenny. It's best if his close relatives don't turn up and give the officials someone to hold for questioning.'

'What are you planning?' she asked, feeling everything getting out of control. 'Are you going to bribe him out of the country? That might backfire! It——' She twisted around in the seat and looked back at Zeb. He looked tired suddenly. All morning he had seemed relaxed and at times actually cheerful. Trust, she thought, and she saw the slight frown that emphasised the lines around his mouth.

Neil was laughing, his amusement booming out as his eyes caught his brother's in the rear-view mirror. 'My big brother, the family rock, sneaking around Mexico, contemplating bribing officials and—I'm saving this memory.' He was grinning gleefully as he jumped a stop sign and turned a corner to the shouted curse of a Mexican taxi driver. 'Thank you, Misty, for getting him into this! Some day when Zeb's looking his stodgiest, I can look him in the eye and laugh, and he'll know exactly what I'm thinking about!'

Zeb said curtly, 'Stow it!' and Neil fell silent, although Misty could see his lips twitching.

She was not sure that it was funny. She swallowed. 'Will you be careful?' she asked shakily, talking to both of them. Kenny had got himself into this, but Zeb and Neil had not asked for trouble. Zeb was doing this for her. He must care for her, too, because Neil was right. This was far from the kind of behaviour one would expect from the president of Turner Enterprises. And Neil—Neil must be doing it for his brother. 'Please don't get yourself into anything that—— Whatever it costs you, I'll see that Kenny pays it back.'

'One thing at a time,' said Zeb. He had said those words last night, and again this morning. Her fingers went to her lips, touching them, remembering. She flushed with the memory, her body stirring again with desire and need, her lips parting unconsciously.

Their worlds were opposite in so many ways. She knew that it was this very difference that attracted her, her yearning for solid stability even while she enjoyed the wild challenge of her erratic occupation. And she thought that perhaps Zeb was attracted by the wild part of her, as if it fascinated him in the same way his stability drew her. But in the end would he not go back to Alice, who belonged to his world?

She was silent on the flight to Los Frailes, unable to appreciate the beauty of the country. At the small airport Neil found someone with a car who was willing to rent it for a day. They headed for the beach, stopping twice on the way to put water in the radiator of the car.

They found the caravan was nestled against a big fig tree, half concealed from the road, as the doctor had told them. The wind had blown hard constantly, driving the sand up around the caravan until the wheels had disappeared. The road itself was merely a wide, sandy path between cactus and palm trees. Everything was sand and sun and wind.

Beyond the caravan the road faded out into a wide, sweeping curve that was the beach at Los Frailes. There were a few people far off on the beach, some temporary buildings on the sand and two Mexican men talking to a girl in a bikini. Two tents were hidden in the trees, a truck with Alaska licence-plates beside one of them. Five sail-boats were anchored out in the bay.

'I'll wait in the car,' said Neil.

Zeb reached the caravan first and rapped briskly on the door. There was no answer, no voice from inside. He tried the knob and it turned. Misty bit her lip, wondering how Kenny would react when Zeb came through the door, but he stepped back, did not actually open the door.

'You, I think, Misty,' he said quietly.

She nodded. She could not talk. She got her hand on the knob, stopped and worried her lip with her teeth. Zeb's hand gripped her shoulder and she turned to look up a query. He bent and took her lips in a swift, hard kiss. It was easier to open the door, easier to tell herself she did not know why she would be afraid to walk in.

Inside, the caravan was furnished comfortably, fitted with stove and refrigerator, sofa and chair. In the back she could see a bed, but it was made up and looked too tidy for Kenny to have used it.

He was on the sofa, propped up and staring at her. She had never seen him like this before, unshaven and weak, his face tired, dissolute and lined, and older than his body.

'Hi,' she said finally. She saw his jaw work. He hated this. His leg was bandaged and propped up on a pillow. She saw two empty beer bottles beside the sofa and wondered how much he'd had to drink. He had always hidden his drinking from her, although she knew he did it. 'How are you?' She wished the words unsaid as soon as her lips formed them. The answer was obvious.

'Been better,' he growled, frowning at the spot behind her. 'What the hell is *he* doing here?'

She dug her hands deeper into the pockets of her jacket. She was frightened to look back, to see what might be in Zeb's face. She swallowed. Damn it! Maybe he'd got himself into a stupid mess here in Mexico, and he drank too much, but he was her uncle and she loved him.

Behind her, Zeb's voice came, easy and controlled. What was he thinking? 'I'm Zeb Turner. I came down with Misty, to help her.'

If Kenny were on his feet he would probably be just an inch or two shy of Zeb's height, although she knew that wouldn't intimidate her uncle. There was a long silence and she felt herself tensing again. Kenny wasn't going to throw a temper fit, was he?

'Kenny——' she began, her voice unusually sharp.

But he was laughing, his face a wry distortion of humour. He must be in pain from the leg, although she knew he would never admit it. He was giving all his attention to Zeb now. 'To help her,' he repeated with some kind of inexplicable enjoyment. 'Not to help me?' He frowned, then said roughly, 'I don't need help from your kind.'

Zeb passed her, pulled a chair up and sat backwards in it with his arms crossed on its back. 'You've got the *federales* looking for you and your leg smashed up. You can't walk, you can't go through the border, and you're dependent on a friendly doctor to send you your food. I'd say you need help.'

'So?' The aggressiveness in Kenny's voice was, she knew, a direct result of his frustration at being helpless. 'Is it your business?'

Zeb nodded, his voice very matter-of-fact. 'If it's Misty's business, then it's mine. I might be able to straighten things out, but first I need to know what you've actually done.'

Misty saw the nerve twitch in Kenny's eyelid. He seemed to be trying to stare Zeb down, but it didn't work. He said finally, 'Misty can get me out without——'

'No!' Kenny's eyes jerked to her. She swallowed. 'Kenny there's no way I can drive you back to San Diego. The doctor said you shouldn't let your leg be jolted that much. I—we're going to do it Zeb's way. Trust him, Kenny!'

'Do you?' Kenny's eyes seemed to bore into hers, reminding her of another time, another man who had simply not been worth her love or her trust.

She pushed her hands into her pockets, as she said, 'Yes, and you'd better, too, or else I'm walking out and you can get yourself out of the country.' She took a deep breath and found herself bursting with a hot anger that she had not known was there. 'Kenny, you've no right to ask me to try to smuggle you out of here if there's any other possible way.'

He seemed to sag into the sofa. 'No right in any case,' he said in a tired voice. 'But I was just too wiped to work my way out of it.' She bit her lip. She wanted to go to him, to touch him, to tell him she had not meant any harsh words. They had never hugged and kissed, not since those old days so dimly remembered, before...

Before what? Why had she never known, never been told? Zeb leaned forward and started asking Kenny questions, and she realised that she had spoken sharply to Kenny for the first time in her life. Until now, she supposed she had been too afraid to risk whatever affection he felt for her to speak her mind to him.

The story Zeb drew out was rather tawdry, although nothing in Zeb's face showed if he felt distaste. Kenny had driven down Baja, then gone to the mainland by ferry, taking his car with him on a temporary import permit. Under the terms of the permit it was forbidden for him to sell the car, but he had got into some heavy drinking and run out of money.

'Why didn't you wire me for money?' Misty asked, but he did not answer and she remembered the collect telephone call from Mexico.

He had sold the car, then somehow become involved in an accident while he was still in the car. Apparently he had asked the new owner to give him a ride. To the bar, Misty assumed. The accident had turned into a mess, a legal nightmare. No one but Kenny was hurt, but the police appeared and started enquiring into ownership.

Kenny grimaced. 'Damned foolish, I know,' he said uncomfortably. He was not looking at Misty, and seemed to find it easier to talk to Zeb. 'I was loaded, and not thinking clearly when I sold it. It hit me pretty hard when the accident happened. Other car damaged. Insurance invalid, I'm sure, because he had a bill of sale from me and he wasn't insured, hadn't had time yet. On the other hand, I probably wasn't insured either. Damage to the other vehicle, and me higher than a kite and in violation of lord knows how many regulations, aside from selling that car, which I suppose qualifies as some kind of smuggling.'

Kenny strained himself up into a sitting position. 'I got out of there, found a taxi and got to the waterfront, found a yachtie down there on a sail-boat. He was sailing over to Baja the next morning and that seemed a hell of a lot better place to be, so I bummed a ride and some bandages out of his first-aid kit.' He subsided back against the pillows, shrugging and finally smiling his old smile. 'One whopping mess, eh, Misty?'

'A whopper,' she agreed, unable to stop herself from smiling back. 'One day they're going to hang you. None too soon, either.'

'Yeah, well . . .' His eyes closed, and she could see the heavy lines of pain and exhaustion on his face. She looked across and met Zeb's eyes.

The man she loved said softly to her, 'And you think I put up with too much from Helen?' And somehow, amazingly, there was laughter in his eyes. She found herself laughing, too, and Kenny's eyes flew open.

'So you're not going to throw me to the wolves?' murmured Kenny.

'Not this time,' said Zeb, standing up, suddenly formal and very tall. 'I'll need your passport and your tourist card. There's not much time if we want to get this straightened out today.'

Her uncle frowned and she said sharply, 'Where are they?' Kenny was going to argue. She could see it in his eyes and that stubborn set to his mouth. She looked around, spotted the light carry-all he often used when he was travelling.

'Misty!' Kenny's voice was sharp, commanding. It had always terrified her when he'd shouted like that, but she ignored it. The bag was not locked and she opened it, found the passport in the inside pocket. His tourist card was inside. She handed them to Zeb and he caught her hand in his.

'Come outside with me,' he asked quietly. She nodded and he led her out, his hand still holding hers. Kenny watched them go, an angry resentment radiating from his helpless form. Outside, she leaned back against the closed door. Zeb stood in front of her, one arm stretched out to the door just at her shoulder, the other catching her chin. 'OK?' he asked gently.

She licked her lips uneasily. The wind was blowing in off the water, sweeping her hair back and drying her lips. 'I—Zeb, aren't you wishing you'd never got...involved with me?'

He bent and possessed her lower lip as her teeth worried it. 'No,' he said, and his voice was not loud or forceful, but there was no doubt he meant it. 'You're the best thing that has ever happened in my life.' She frowned, but her heart was singing as he asked, 'Are you OK here while I go back with Neil and try to straighten out this mess?'

She nodded, and he said wryly, 'If you get the urge to tell him a few home truths while I'm gone, don't resist too hard, will you?'

She giggled, then her grin faded and she was not sure that it was funny. 'I know he's awful when he's at his worst, but—he's not always like this, and——'

Amazingly, he smiled, and her uneasiness shrank to nothing as he said, 'Darling, I'm very good at handling difficult relatives. I've been doing it for years.' His hands possessed her arms and he said softly, 'You know, he loves you very much.' She shook her head slightly, but Zeb's voice was so sure. 'He's rotten at showing it, but it was in his eyes. He hated telling that tale with you there, making you think badly of him.'

'No, I——' She blinked and felt the moisture in her eyes, and knew that it must be true if Zeb said it was. 'I didn't know that. There's a lot I don't understand.' She frowned, worrying at the past with a new perspective. His hands squeezed briefly, then he stepped back. His voice was very low. She had to strain to catch the words.

'If you need telling, Misty...' He cleared his throat, then said with uncharacteristic impatience, 'Somehow I'm terrified to tell you this, Misty Dawn, but I love you too.'

Then he was gone, the old car rocking as it made new tracks in the road that was almost not a road at all; and she was left leaning against the trailer, weak and shaky and feeling the singing joy growing inside herself. He loved her. Love, and if Zeb said the word it meant everything. She felt the wind against her face, slowly became aware of two small children staring at her. They were clad in shorts, were barefoot, and had wide, curious eyes.

'Hi,' she said breathlessly. The small boy turned and ran away towards the water through the sand. The girl, about six or seven, remained staring at Misty.

'Is he gonna marry you?' asked the girl solemnly.

'I don't know.' She brushed her lips and remembered his touch with an intensity that was overwhelming. Inside her, an ache was growing for the time when they could stand alone together and deal with what had happened between them.

One thing at a time. Kenny first. She turned and left the little girl, opened the door to the caravan and stepped in.

'He gone?' asked Kenny sourly.

'Yes.' She walked past him to the little kitchen area. There was food in the cupboards. She took out tins, frowned at the labels. 'I don't suppose you've eaten today?' The doctor had said his daughter lived in the nearby village and that she came each evening to give the invalid *cena*. She took down a tin of soup, lined up a tin of beans beside it. She was avoiding facing Kenny. Outside, just now, Zeb had said he loved her and her heart was swelling to bursting, but she had not spoken the words inside her yet. She should have shouted after him, shouldn't she?

I love you, darling!

She had to learn how to do that, to open her lips and tell the people she loved what she felt. Kenny should learn, too, because she and her uncle had gone a whole lifetime circling around each other, avoiding anything personal or private—crazy, when they had always been two people alone with only each other.

'I suppose I haven't seen the back of him?'

She heard Kenny's growl and found herself smiling as she opened a tin and discovered that what she had thought was tomato soup was actually some kind of puree tomatoes. She put it aside and picked up the tin of beans, saying firmly, 'No, you haven't. You're going to see a lot of him.'

She lifted a sombrero-shaped lid from a small wicker holder and found corn tortillas inside. 'I can offer you tortillas and refried beans. That do?'

'Beef steak,' his voice came back sulkily. 'I want beef steak.'

Difficult relatives. She grinned and opened the tin of beans. There was a gas stove, a saucepan. She found a big frying pan and heated the tortillas. She was no cook, but it was impossible to mess up this drab meal. She found some *naranja* in the refrigerator and poured him a glass of the orange juice.

'Mexican food,' she announced. Kenny liked eating Mexican, and tortillas and beans were surely Mexican, but when she pulled the chair over beside him and set the steaming plate on it he groaned. 'Eat,' she said. 'It's all you're going to get.'

'What about you? I'll share.'

'Forget it. I had lunch.' She sat down in another straight-backed chair. Except for the sofa, there was nothing comfortable here to sit in. 'No, I didn't have lunch,' she realised, and found herself reaching for a tortilla.

When she cleaned away the dishes after their plain meal, she could feel the air filled with words unsaid. All her life it had been that way, the words never spoken. She put the dishes in the sink, and decided that she would wash them later. She went back to Kenny and her heart was pounding hard.

'Uncle Kenny, I——' He stilled. It was years since she had called him by anything but his first name. His eyes were already shearing away from her. She felt her legs trembling, pulled the chair a little away from the sofa and sat down, facing him and hugging herself with her crossed arms. 'I want you to tell me about my parents.'

She saw that look in his eyes as they sheared past her. It had been the same that day so many years ago, when he had walked out and she had thought there was no one left in the world for her. He would run away now, if he could, but his leg had him trapped.

'I know you don't want to tell me,' she said gently. 'I—I need to know what happened. I dream about it and I don't know. Not knowing is more frightening than the reality could ever be.'

It was scary, watching his eyes unwilling to meet hers. He might never look at her again, might never let her share even the cool relationship they had. She loosened her arms and found her hands in her hair, pushing it back, and he growled, 'If you wanted to know, why didn't you go look it up? I figured by now you would have.'

'No.' She had been afraid to, afraid to find out whatever Kenny did not want to tell her. It would have been a betrayal of him somehow if she had sneaked behind him to search out the truth he could not tell her. 'I wanted you to tell me.'

He struggled up and fought with the pillows behind him, and she knew that he did not want her to come and help. She should not be sitting like this, staring at him. He needed room, needed to hide what was in his face.

'Coffee,' he said abruptly, and she stood up.

'I'll see if there's any.' In the little kitchen area she filled a kettle and turned on the gas, and hoped the noises reassured him. She could not see him. He was hidden by the back of the sofa.

'I wanted them to go out and see this property I was gonna buy.' His voice was uneasy, the memories thickening it. 'It was a ranch, and I was going to be Roy Rogers or something, I guess. I was tired of being in the police force, tired of crazy policies and bosses. It was an overnight trip. Your mom asked a neighbour to come and stay with you.'

She tried to remember the neighbour, but couldn't.

'Larry, your dad, thought it was a crazy idea. We drove down there, and he said the property would flood in the first heavy rain, and I'd have nothing but misery with it. We argued about it. Your mom tried to get us to stop, but we always fought like that, had ever since we were kids. I was the younger and smaller, and he was always the winner.' Misty thought he shrugged, although she could not see him. There would be a self-mocking smile on his face, hiding the pain. 'It never meant anything. I think we kind of enjoyed our arguments, although she never understood that. Larry said she was an only child and just didn't understand brothers fighting. He loved her very much.'

She swallowed the lump in her throat and turned off the gas under the steaming kettle. Instant coffee in the cupboard. She fumbled and found two cups. Zeb, she thought. If I didn't know I had Zeb coming back to hold me, this would be too much, too shattering.

'What happened?' It was her voice, although she was not aware that she spoke.

'We stopped at a pub, argued more. I drank too much. Then we went to the car, and Larry was insisting on driving and Pam was begging me to let him, and I wouldn't. I don't remember all of that. All I remember was the rain, and the lights on the highway ahead, and Pam screaming when I went into a skid. I think—I don't know the rest. I woke up in the hospital and I was the only damned one that had nothing, no injury. I had a hell of a hangover.' He groaned and said, 'I've still got a bloody hangover.'

She picked up the kettle, but there was no way she could pour the water. It settled back on to the stove with a bang and she went to him, found him looking grey and pale. He might have looked much like this in that hospital when he'd woken up and found out what he had done.

'They tried me,' he said harshly, his words holding her away. 'Manslaughter. I was guilty. Of course I was guilty.'

She sat down beside him, her body pressing against his, and he cringed away from her. 'Kenny, where was I when this was happening?' Trials took time. There was waiting and worrying and agony. She had been alone, abandoned, and he had been alone, too. It made no sense, when they could have had each other.

'I sent you to that school. I would have taken you home with me, but I thought I'd be in gaol and it seemed better...and...I felt guilty just looking at you.' He shrugged and he had nowhere to look, no way to escape her. She heard a bird call outside, and someone shouted. Kenny said, 'They suspended my sentence.'

'But you didn't suspend anything.' She touched him, and she did not let herself draw back when his face tried to shut her out. 'You've been punishing yourself ever since.' She thought of her own loneliness, her insecurities, and knew she could not add to his punishment by telling him how he had hurt her. 'I'm sorry,' she whispered, and whether he liked it or not she threw herself into his arms and stopped trying to keep the tears back.

CHAPTER TEN

ZEB found her sitting on the sandy slope that led down to the water. He sat down beside her and took her hand in his.

'How did you make out?' she asked.

'All right.' He shifted in the sand, making himself comfortable, and assured her, 'It's all right.' Then he touched her cheek. 'You've been crying. What's wrong?'

He looked worried. She remembered that look on his face yesterday when he had crouched down beside her at the telephone in her house. She had been terrified, frightened for Kenny, and Zeb had been watching her, worried...about her. He could keep his cool while he handled the rest of them, his sneaky brother and his clinging mother, his teenage nephews and even her screwball uncle...but Misty was somehow different. She lifted her hand and touched his cheek too, felt the slight roughness.

'I didn't pack a razor,' he said wryly.

She smiled. 'I thought you were always so well-organised, that I was the one who acted without thinking.'

His fingers linked with hers and he said, 'You're actually pretty cautious; you just don't look it.'

'How can you say that when you just stopped me from smuggling Kenny out of Mexico?'

'I know, but that's different.' He was playing with her fingers, concentrating on them, saying, 'You'd do anything for Max or for Kenny.'

He was staring at her hand as if he were afraid to look into her eyes. She whispered, 'And for you. I'd do anything for you if you needed me.' She swallowed and held her breath, and in the second's silence she had time to fear that he had regretted telling her he loved her, that he would turn and she would see it in his eyes. She said hurriedly, 'Kenny? What—it's all right about Kenny?'

His fingers gripped hard, briefly, 'I think we've got it worked out. Of course, he has to take the car back. Well, actually, I've arranged for someone to go over to the mainland and bring it up to San Diego.'

'The man who paid for it——'

'He gets his money back. That's looked after, too.' She frowned, adding up a driver to San Diego and an unknown amount reimbursed to the man who had tried to buy the car. Zeb said, 'Don't worry about it, Misty. I'll get it out of him.'

She turned to face him. He had been staring out over the ocean, and he turned when she did. She thought she recognised the look in his eyes and her nervousness faded. 'You're going to look after it for me? I'm not to worry, or count up what he owes you, or——'

'That's right.' He was frowning, troubled again. She wondered why he thought he loved her when she disturbed his equilibrium so much. He asked, 'Do you mind?'

She shook her head. 'No, but I think you should make him pay you back. I know the state of his bank account, and it could take a while, but he shouldn't get away with this, you shouldn't pay.' He was frowning and she said, 'Zeb, he'll do it again. I know him, and it'll happen again and again, and he'll be like a teenager who won't grow up.'

'OK, but let me look after it.' He touched her hair, his fingers threading through the windblown curls, finding the tingling awareness of her scalp. 'I want to make love to you again,' he said huskily. 'Did you know that?'

'Yes.' She licked lips that had turned suddenly dry, felt her breasts rising to aching awareness, as if he had touched them. She asked, 'Kenny? What about Kenny?'

'Neil's going to fly him home in the Lear. The paperwork's all clear, and Neil's up there getting Kenny into the car.'

She stumbled to her feet, Zeb's hand steadying her in the sand, and suddenly it was happening too soon. The jet was fast, and they would be in San Diego long before night fell. The world would press in around them and she was terrified that, if she did not get the chance to tell him soon, she would never manage to get those words out.

I love you. The words did not come, and then they were at the car.

'Well?' said Neil, his hands on his hips, his legs astride as he stood beside the car. Kenny was inside, sitting sideways in the back seat with his leg propped up. He looked disgruntled. Neil looked at Zeb. 'All set? We'd better get a move on. I'll fly you to Ensenada to pick up your car, shall I?' Neil laughed. 'I don't think you and Misty should leave the country without the car. There've been enough irregularities already. I'll get the private eye here to his doctor in San Diego, tuck him in and call the secretary lady.'

Kenny wailed from inside the car, 'Don't call Jo-Anne!'

'Yes,' said Misty. 'Yes, call her. I'll give you her phone number, and she'll look after everything.' Kenny groaned, and she wondered how she could have missed that there was something between Kenny and his secretary, whether the two of them knew it or not.

She started around the car to the passenger door. Then she stopped as she realised, 'I left the dirty dishes in there. After the doctor was good enough to loan this caravan to Kenny. I can't just leave it——'

Kenny said, 'Actually, the caravan belongs to the doctor's daughter and her husband. They said they won't need it for a couple of weeks at least.' Misty realised that there was quite a bit to the story that she did not know yet. How had Kenny found the doctor and the caravan? Had the boat landed him on the beach here? Had the skipper gone to the village for help?

She missed something. Neil was saying, 'What? Did I hear that right?' She stopped, staring across the roof of the car at Zeb. He looked embarrassed, like a small boy caught in an illicit adventure.

'Say it again,' said Neil, grinning.

'You heard.' Zeb frowned, then grinned, his eyes flying across the car to hers, then shearing away almost shyly. 'It's my turn,' he told his brother wryly. 'You made a damned idiot of yourself flying all over the continent, and I never even laughed. Now, will you get the hell out of here?'

Neil drawled, 'Well, I——' but something in Zeb's eyes must have warned him because he said abruptly, 'OK, I'm on my way. I can't miss a chance to turn your tidy shipyard upside-down.' The engine roared, sputtered, then smoothed into something that would hopefully get them to the little airport. 'When you get home, you won't recognise the place,' said Neil.

From the back seat, through the open window, Kenny said, 'Take care, Misty Dawn. Don't hurry home.'

Somehow it had been decided that she and Zeb were not going in the car. Confused, she bent down to the window and Kenny growled at her, 'If you let him get away, you're a fool.'

She smiled tremulously. 'I'm not that much of a fool.'

Then the car was gone and there was nothing between Misty and Zeb except ten feet of dusty, sandy road and a silence that seemed to stretch forever. The wind and the trees stilled, and the sun beat down from a clear blue sky. Even the sound of the surf rolling in on the sandy beach seemed to die away to nothing. There was only Zeb in the world.

'I'll help you with the dishes,' he offered. His face was very still, very blank, and she knew that look now. He was every bit as nervous as she was. Later she would tell him about Kenny's confession, but right now there were more important things for them to talk about.

She managed to come to the middle of the road. Someone came out of the blue tent that was erected beside the big cactus. Neither Misty nor Zeb noticed him. She asked, 'Are you any good at doing dishes?'

'Fair. I'm better at cooking steaks.' He was not smiling.

'I haven't really had the chance to enjoy one of your steaks.' They had fought, and he had walked out of the door. She touched his chest lightly, fleetingly until his hand came up and trapped hers against him. She offered, 'I make a great meal of refried beans.'

'I hate refried beans, but for you I'll eat them.' He turned her hand and possessed it with his. 'The car's gone and we're here—I didn't ask you if you would stay here with me. I did it again, you know. Manipulating you. Did you want to go with them?'

'No.' She twisted her fingers into his, caught his other hand and stood looking up at him in the middle of the road. She whispered, 'I kind of liked it. I didn't want to go back yet. I was afraid that... You asked Neil to look after the shipyard for you?' He nodded and she said, 'Have you ever done that before?'

'Never. You know damned well I haven't.' He jerked as a horn blared, and suddenly there was a truck, easing along the road, the driver laughing, shouting, 'Hey, move it somewhere else, children!'

Misty was still flushed a wild red when Zeb pushed the door to the caravan closed behind them. He reached back to the door and she saw his hand fasten the lock, then he turned back and the world was really gone, shut out and only the two of them inside. He said raggedly, 'There are too many damned people around here. We're in the middle of nowhere in southern Baja. Wouldn't you think we could be alone for five bloody minutes?'

She hugged herself, saw his eyes fasten on her lower lip and realised she was chewing it. 'I didn't think you were the kind of man who used profanities.'

'I wasn't.' He pushed his hand through his hair and she smiled when it lost its tidiness and became unruly. 'I was organised and my life was very tidy, very tame.'

She frowned, suddenly frightened, and he said, 'Dull. I love my family, and I like running the shipyard, but a man needs something else in his life.' He gulped, then said, 'I love you, Misty Dawn, and I want you to share your life with me.'

One step. Two. She was standing in front of him and he did not reach out yet, as if there was something she had to do first. She knew what, but the words were hard. She said nervously, 'You know, my bag is still in the plane, on its way to San Diego.'

He nodded, his lips curving up slightly. 'Mine, too. Is it that hard to say, Misty?' He reached for her, but his fingers curled in on themselves and he pulled his hand back before he touched her. 'I know you love me, Misty Dawn. I know you're scared, but I promise you it will be all right.'

She stared at the third button of his shirt. 'Aren't you afraid Neil will do all sorts of things you wouldn't like if you send him up there to look after the shipyard?'

'He probably won't. He won't have time, looking after his operation and mine, and trying to spend time with Serena and Keith and get ready for the wedding.' He frowned, admitted, 'Yeah, it makes me nervous.'

Her hands were dug into the pockets of the jacket again, fingers torturing a piece of lint she found in the lining of the pocket. She whispered, 'Zeb, are you wishing you had gone back with Neil?'

'No, darling.' He sounded exasperated. She worried her lower lip again, wished she were not being such an idiot. He sighed and said, 'I suppose we should do those dishes?' He looked across to the little kitchen area, his eyes resigned.

Then she said in a rush, 'I love you,' because he was going to wait forever if he had to, and she didn't want to do that to him. He was very still, did not turn back to her. She cleared her throat. 'Did you hear me?'

'Yeah.' He smiled, and his eyes found hers. 'I think so. Or maybe I dreamed it. Was it that hard to say?'

'Yes...no.' She ground her fists deep into the pockets. 'Are you just going to stare at me?' Maybe he was. She could do all sorts of difficult things as part of her job. Surely she could manage this? She swallowed, stepped closer. He was very tall. She spread her hands on his chest, feeling his firm maleness through the thin tropical shirt. She had to go on tiptoes to nestle her moist kiss against his neck.

His voice was ragged. 'If I do just stand here, will you make love to me? I'd like that.'

She slipped her arms up around his neck and pulled his head down so that her lips could capture his. She felt him shudder, heard his low groan, then his arms circled her and he was holding her close, fitting every curve of her woman's body to his hard maleness, until she gasped and her eyes drooped with passion, her lips opened, searching the intimacy of his deep, sensuous kiss.

He lifted his head a long time later, looking down at her as if she were the most precious thing in his world. She leaned back in his arms, and found her thighs excitingly close to his. His grip shifted down to her hips and the intimacy was shattering. She trembled in his arms, felt his hard response.

He growled, 'Do you really want to do the dishes?'

'Don't you think we should?' She saw the frown, the disappointment in his eyes, then she shifted and felt his need, more demanding against her. She admitted softly, 'I'd rather make love with you.'

She could feel his desire, see it in his eyes. Yet his hands were stilled on her, his eyes golden as they looked down at her. Finally he said, 'Tell me what's bothering you. What is it that you aren't saying to me, darling?'

She swallowed. 'No, I——' How had he known? She'd been pushing it back, telling herself it was all right, but afraid it wasn't. Now she admitted it to him and to herself, 'I—I love you. I—but I can't—if—Zeb, I can't share you with Alice.'

His lips took hers, his tongue possessing, plundering her to her depths. She was pliant in his arms, then stirring, her lips and hands and heated flesh seeking and giving. 'I was scared,' she admitted. 'I was afraid that if I told you that——'

'You should have known better.' He picked her up easily in his arms, and she found herself lowered on to the bed, Zeb coming down beside her. 'I guess I just assumed you knew—the way you told me about my life that first night in the pool. You knew about Julian and Mother and Alice. You seemed to know everything, and no one who knew about Alice and I could think there was anything in it but friendship. I'm not saying we weren't lovers, but...' his hand stroked her hip and accepted the thrust of her body as it stirred against his '... we weren't lovers like this. No one was ever like this for me.' He laughed, but it turned to a low lover's growl. 'You sure as hell knew how you affected me that first night.' She had a vivid vision of that night, Zeb standing on the deck of the spa looking at her, his desire unmistakable.

Her eyes were closed, her face turned into his shoulder as she admitted, 'You shook me up that night. I hadn't let myself think about a man that way since Wayne. And he'd never made me feel like that. No one but you ever looked at me and made me feel that I was someone special, that the world was warm and beautiful.'

He stilled, touched her face, and she opened her eyes and stared up at him. 'I saw her the day of the AGM,' he said soberly. 'You wouldn't have lunch with me, and I knew when you walked out of that boardroom that I had to keep you in my life somehow. That meeting was— with you there, it was like there was light in everything. An extra spark, my whole world was alive. When you walked out of the room that light went with you. I went to find Alice, to tell her that I hoped she would still be my friend, but that we wouldn't be seeing each other as lovers again.'

How could he have known so quickly? She touched his face, felt the lines smooth as she stroked them. The slight roughness of his beard gave him an uncharacter-istic untidiness that made her smile. 'I was terrified of you,' she admitted. 'You weren't supposed to get past the official Misty Donovan, the one in the office. You kept getting under my guard. No man ever got into my house, but you did. You even got Max to smile at you... Max!'

She jerked, trying to sit up, but his body prevented her, his hand stroking the long curve of her hip as she twisted to her side. 'He'll be fine. If I can trust the shipyard to Neil, you can trust your dog to Jo-Anne.'

'Kenny and Max hate each other,' she worried.

Zeb grinned. 'Is Kenny going to be sleeping at Jo-Anne's?'

'Oh! No, I guess not—maybe.' She shared a smile with him, as if they had a secret. 'He'll be at her mercy, won't he?' She let herself relax to his touch, watched as her fingers unfastened two of his shirt buttons, then a third.

'You're getting better at that.' He caught her hand as it slipped under his shirt. She could see the fire in his eyes, but his fingers held hers still. 'Jo-Anne will look after Max. She'll tell him you'll be home soon and she won't let him worry too much.' He sounded serious, as if Max would understand the words. She blinked, be-mused, and wondered if that were possible.

She touched his lips and felt them tremble, and knew that he was afraid to ask what was in his eyes. Whatever it was, she would give it to him. Anything. She turned her body and pulled herself against him, her arms around his neck. 'I love you,' she whispered. 'I'll try to be whatever you want.'

'My wife.' The words sounded harsh, then he cleared his throat and said, 'That's what I want. I want to love, honour and cherish you . . . forever. I want you in my life and my home and—if it's what you want, too, I want us to have children, our children.'

He felt her tension. 'What is it?' His lips brushed hers fleetingly, then he drew back. She could see the gold in his eyes turning brown and uneasy.

'It's your house,' she admitted finally. 'I'll—I don't think I can live in that house. I—it terrifies me. It's big and dark and—I felt as if I was on trial, and your ancestors were going to fail me, burn me at the stake more likely. I——'

She gasped as he hugged her hard, then their lips were entangled and he said, 'You crazy lady! I told you, I hate the damned house myself. And I told you before that I want to share your house with you.'

'Isn't it too small?' She could see him there and she wanted to share it with him. 'Can we? Where could we put Keith?'

'We can add to it, but Keith's going to have to stay with his grandmother for at least a while because I need you to myself. Later he can come to us.'

Us. She glowed, settled into his arms, then worried, 'Will he mind? Maybe Keith won't want to have me for an aunt, and——'

Zeb laughed. 'He's nuts about you. He been telling me ever since the night you stayed that I'd better marry you, that with you for an aunt and Serena for a stepmother he'll have it made.'

'Oh.' It was a strange idea, having a husband and a nephew. Neil would be her brother. She liked the idea, but hoped she could like Serena. It sounded fantastic. A big family, and the man she loved. The kind of future dreams were made of. 'But what about your swimming pool? You go swimming every night and——'

'Have you ever heard of swimming in the ocean?' She frowned, and he said, 'Misty, do you want to marry me or not?' and she heard his voice suddenly frightened and vulnerable.

'Yes,' she whispered, then her voice came strong. 'Oh, yes! It—I—oh, yes, please, darling!' He had said they could add to the house. She closed her eyes and saw it. Rooms for the children and for Keith, two children running along the beach and Zeb walking behind them, his hand holding hers.

The gold lights in his eyes flickered and she said softly, 'I want all of it. I want you and the kids and the extra rooms built on and... But I might alienate the rest of your family the way I did Helen. What if——'

'You were right about Helen.'

'What?' She succeeded in sitting up on the bed, free of his caressing hands. She realised then that her blouse was gaping open, her jacket pushed back off her shoulders. Absently, she shed the jacket, let it fall to the floor. 'What do you mean, I was right? You were furious with me.'

'I was wrong.' He stretched out on the bed, one arm behind his head, his other hand catching the edge of her unbuttoned blouse and drawing it away from her breast. 'You wore a bra today.'

She felt the silky fabric sliding down her arms. She moved her arm and let the blouse join the jacket. He followed every movement. She saw him lick his lips, and her breasts seemed to swell so that she had a crazy moment thinking they would burst out of her bra. She reached down and finished unbuttoning his shirt, concentrating hard on the task, then smoothing it away from his muscular chest. She smoothed her fingers along the pale skin where the sun seldom reached, found his eyes and watched the pupils contract as she explored the ridges and valleys of his muscles.

'I love the feel of you,' she admitted brazenly, and she felt his chest and knew that his heart crashed against his ribs. 'What do you mean, you were wrong about Helen?' She realised that she didn't give a damn about Helen, not with her love lying there wanting her.

'I love the look of you,' he murmured. 'That bra is sexy as hell. Why do you own underwear like that if you don't want a man in your life?'

She reached up and released the catch to the bra, and he stopped breathing, then he was strong and sure and his hands slid the lacy undergarment out of their way. She shivered, sitting above him, his eyes taking in every curve, his hand reaching towards her when he saw her nipples swell and harden with desire.

'Helen,' she reminded him, but the word was hardly understandable. She could hardly breathe. Soon his fingers would touch...caressing...gentle...soft fire roaring everywhere. Whatever was holding her upright was draining away. She swayed and her eyelids drooped, then his hands were holding her and she gave herself up to them.

He held her still, not close to him, his eyes flaring, promising that he could not wait much longer either. She felt the heady excitement pounding in her, anticipation growing as they deliberately teased each other, holding fulfilment just out of reach...for just one moment more.

'Helen,' he said. 'She phoned Neil last week.' Her mind was three words behind his voice. She slid her hands along his chest, leaned down and let his strength support her weight, felt the ragged difficulty of his words as he said, 'She's looking for a job... said she realised when you bawled her out that... Oh, Misty! I——'

There were no more words, only the murmurs of love, the touch and heat of lips and hands and their two warm, loving bodies... the man and the woman, pledging their love, their union of mind and body... forever.

2 NEW TITLES FOR JANUARY 1990

Mariah *by Sandra Canfield is the first novel in a sensational quartet of sisters in search of love...* Mariah's sensual and provocative behaviour contrasts enigmatically with her innocent and naive appearance... Only the maverick preacher can recognise her true character and show her the way to independence and true love.

£2.99

Faye is determined to make a success of the farm she has inherited – but she hadn't accounted for the bitter battle with neighbour, Seth Carradine, who was after the land himself. In desperation she turns to him for help, and an interesting bargain is struck. **Kentucky Woman** by Casey Douglas, bestselling author of Season of Enchantment. **£2.99**

W☉RLDWIDE

Available from Boots, Martins, John Menzies, W.H. Smith, Woolworths and other paperback stockists.

DESPERADO – Helen Conrad   £2.75

In this fast-paced and compelling novel, jewel thief and embezzler, Michael Drayton, has a five thousand dollar price on his head. With Jessie MacAllister after the reward and hot on his trail, the Desperado turns on his devasting charm, leaving her with one key dilemma... how to turn him in!

ONCE AND FOR ALWAYS
Stella Cameron   £2.99

The magic and beauty of Wales and the picturesque fishing village, Tenby, form the backdrop to Stella Cameron's latest poignant novel. Caitlin McBride's past reads like a fairytale, and returning to Tenby seems to offer the only escape from a dead marriage and hellish family life. But would the spell still exist – and would she find the love she had once left behind?

Published: DECEMBER 1989

W●RLDWIDE

Available from Boots, Martins, John Menzies, W.H. Smith, Woolworths and other paperback stockists.

TASTY FOOD COMPETITION!

How would you like a years supply of Mills & Boon Romances ABSOLUTELY FREE? Well, you can win them! All you have to do is complete the word puzzle below and send it in to us by March. 31st. 1990. The first 5 correct entries picked out of the bag after that date will win **a years supply of Mills & Boon Romances** (*ten books every month - worth £162*) What could be easier?

H	O	L	L	A	N	D	A	I	S	E	R
E	Y	E	G	G	O	W	H	A	O	H	A
R	S	E	E	C	L	A	I	R	U	C	T
B	T	K	K	A	E	T	S	I	F	I	A
E	E	T	I	S	M	A	L	C	F	U	T
U	R	C	M	T	L	H	E	E	L	Q	O
G	S	I	U	T	F	O	N	O	E	D	U
N	H	L	S	O	T	O	N	E	F	M	I
I	S	R	S	O	M	A	C	W	A	A	L
R	I	A	E	E	T	I	R	J	A	E	L
E	F	G	L	L	P	T	O	T	V	R	E
M	O	U	S	S	E	E	O	D	O	C	P

CLAM	HOLLANDAISE	OYSTERS	SPICE
COD	JAM	PRAWN	STEAK
CREAM	LEEK	QUICHE	TART
ECLAIR	LEMON	RATATOUILLE	
EGG	MELON	RICE	PLEASE TURN
FISH	MERINGUE	RISOTTO	OVER FOR
GARLIC	MOUSSE	SALT	DETAILS
HERB	MUSSELS	SOUFFLE	ON HOW
			TO ENTER

HOW TO ENTER

All the words listed overleaf, below the word puzzle, are hidden in the grid. You can find them by reading the letters forward, backwards, up or down, or diagonally. When you find a word, circle it or put a line through it, the remaining letters (which you can read from left to right, from the top of the puzzle through to the bottom) will ask a romantic question.

After you have filled in all the words, don't forget to fill in your name and address in the space provided and pop this page in an envelope (you don't need a stamp) and post it today. Hurry - competition ends March 31st 1990.

Mills & Boon Competition,
FREEPOST,
P.O. Box 236,
Croydon,
Surrey. CR9 9EL

Only one entry per household

Hidden Question _____

_____

Name _____

Address _____

_____

_____

_____ Postcode _____

You may be mailed with other offers as a result of this application.

COMP 8